# The Ruby Dagger
## A Crown Jewels Regency Mystery
### Book 2

Lynn Morrison

Anne Radcliffe

Marketing Chair Press

Copyright © 2024 by Lynn Morrison and Anne Radcliffe

All rights reserved.

No part of this book may be reproduced in any form or by any electronic or mechanical means, including information storage and retrieval systems, without written permission from the authors, except for the use of brief quotations in a book review.

This novel's story and characters are fictitious. Certain long-standing institutions, agencies, and public offices are mentioned, but the story are wholly imaginary. Some of the characters were inspired by actual historical figures, and abide by the generally known facts about these individuals and their relevant time periods. However, their actions and conversations are strictly fiction. All other characters and events are the product of our own imaginations.

Cover design by Melody Simmons

Published by

The Marketing Chair Press, Oxford, England

LynnMorrisonWriter.com

ISBN (paperback): 978-1-7392632-9-4

# Contents

| | |
|---|---|
| Chapter 1 | 1 |
| Chapter 2 | 11 |
| Chapter 3 | 17 |
| Chapter 4 | 25 |
| Chapter 5 | 32 |
| Chapter 6 | 40 |
| Chapter 7 | 47 |
| Chapter 8 | 56 |
| Chapter 9 | 63 |
| Chapter 10 | 71 |
| Chapter 11 | 79 |
| Chapter 12 | 88 |
| Chapter 13 | 95 |
| Chapter 14 | 104 |
| Chapter 15 | 113 |
| Chapter 16 | 121 |
| Chapter 17 | 128 |
| Chapter 18 | 136 |
| Chapter 19 | 145 |
| Chapter 20 | 153 |
| Chapter 21 | 161 |
| Chapter 22 | 168 |
| Chapter 23 | 175 |
| Chapter 24 | 183 |
| Chapter 25 | 189 |
| Chapter 26 | 195 |
| Chapter 27 | 200 |
| Chapter 28 | 208 |
| Chapter 29 | 215 |

| | |
|---|---|
| Historical Notes | 223 |
| Acknowledgments | 227 |
| The Sapphire Intrigue | 229 |
| About Anne Radcliffe | 231 |
| About Lynn Morrison | 233 |
| Also by Lynn Morrison | 235 |

*To Morgan, in thanks for all your help*

# 1

"See the gentleman to the left? That's Lord Harrington. Be sure to acknowledge him; I hear he may be looking for a new wife."

Grace followed the point of her mother's chin, obediently looking in that direction without enthusiasm. Finding the lord in question, she had to stifle the urge to wrinkle her nose. Lord Harrington was fifty if he was a day, and at least two stone heavier than he ought to be.

"It is only my first season, Mama." She left off the remainder of the thought. *I have no cause to be this desperate yet.*

Her mama slanted her a look that spoke volumes, and by now Grace had come to understand her ambitions quite clearly. Deprived of the idea of marrying her daughter to a duke, she was plotting to take every opportunity to find another high-ranking husband for Grace—such as this event at the palace—and her opinion of suitability would make no account for looks or age.

*Or love and friendship*, Grace thought, feeling a hollow space around her heart. *Much less adventure.* Shifting uneasily, she returned her attention to the front of the room.

His Royal Highness the Prince Regent, a king in all but name, sat upon the throne. His mother, Queen Charlotte, stood beside him, the very portrayal of a dutiful wife and mother. Looks could be deceiving, she was reminded. While she knew little of Prinny, those who dared to cross Queen Charlotte's path found her proverbial royal teeth to be as sharp as her wits. She would be surprised to find he was not cut from the same cloth.

On this particular evening, in the throne room of St James's Palace, the prince and queen surveyed the crowd of some fifty attendees, making note of who stood together and which alliances had drifted apart. From the doorway, the Master of Ceremonies raised his voice to announce the arrival of their guest of honour.

"Presenting His Excellency, Baron Gustaf Albin Lindberg, Ambassador of Sweden."

At the back of the room, Lady Grace Tilbury shifted from left to right. No matter where she looked, she could not get a clear view of the doorway. She supposed she should count herself lucky for being in the room at all, but now that she was here, she did not want to miss the ambassador's arrival.

She knew little of the man beyond his name and origin. Tonight marked her opportunity to remedy the gap in her knowledge. She was, however, less interested in the man himself than in the role he occupied. Ambassadors travelled the world and met interesting people. They ventured far beyond the confines of their society with the full blessing of their leaders. Grace could not imagine England appointing a female to such a role, but for this chance, she would be willing to play the role of dutiful wife. *They* frequently accompanied their diplomat husbands on trips, and often played hostess and such.

Not that she had her sights set on marrying the Swedish

ambassador, mind you—but someone like him would be worthy of her consideration. At least she would be able to travel.

With no one behind her, she judged it safe enough to rise on her toes to see if the extra height would provide her with a better vantage point. She barely made it up an inch before her mother pinched her arm.

"*Ow*," Grace mouthed as she rubbed her arm. Her white gloves prevented her from checking whether her mama had left a mark. She cast a glare in her mother's direction and received a hotter one in return.

"Be still!" her mama ordered in a barely audible whisper.

"My view is blocked," Grace explained in an equally low tone.

Lady Tilbury did not roll her eyes, but it was a close thing. She shifted back and motioned for her daughter to swap places with her. Grace slid over until she bumped against her brother Felix, hoping to nudge him aside. He refused to give ground to her, sticking his nose in the air and pretending to ignore her existence.

For all her efforts, Grace discovered her view had improved little. In fact, it might be argued, it had worsened. Although she could now see the ambassador climbing up to the dais to present his gift, she could also see society's most talked about couple of the season. Lady Charity Cresswell—her fastest friend, diamond of the first water, and the queen's favoured debutante—stood beside Lord Roland Percy. Under the flickering flames of the dozens of candles in the chandeliers, Lady Charity's blonde hair gleamed like spun gold. To the casual observer, she appeared as ethereal as any storybook princess. Her society debut, however, had been more like a cautionary tale.

Grace did not allow herself to think overlong about the dark-haired man standing beside her best friend. Lord Roland Percy's military background was evident in his squared shoulders and stiff spine. Visions of him slumped in a hired hansom cab, dressed like a servant, swam to the surface of Grace's memories. She could still remember the touch of his fingers on her face when they had spoken in the Vauxhall maze.

When Charity had been kidnapped, her reputation lay in tatters. It was only because Grace and Roland found her, a fact the queen considered a personal favour, that the results hadn't been worse.

As thanks, Lady Grace and her family now found themselves invited to all the best events. Roland's reward... was an engagement to Charity, the most sought-after debutante of the season. Publicly announced and blessed by the queen herself. Not only would Charity marry into a duchy, this also saved her virtue from certain ruin.

Grace's breath caught at the pain of that thought. She was supposed to be thrilled for her dearest friend, and yet...

Turning her attention, she noticed all eyes were on the ambassador. Baron Lindberg had stepped onto the dais, putting him high enough for Grace to get a clear view. He stood tall and imposing, with sharp, steel-grey eyes that seemed to miss nothing. His hair, once a dark chestnut, was now flecked with silver. He was dressed impeccably in a dark tailored suit with a long tailcoat.

In a deep and measured voice, he addressed the crown prince. "It is my great pleasure to offer your highness this small token of affection, to demonstrate the newfound accord of friendship that binds our great nations." He stepped aside to allow a footman to come forward and present the gift.

After the ceremony came to an end, the group adjourned to the dining room for a formal dinner. Grace and her family were among the last to leave the room, given how far from the door they stood, but the silver lining was that Grace had the chance to linger for an extra moment as they passed the displayed gift.

*The Ruby Dagger*

A velvet cushion, in the palest shade of ivory, with golden braid and tassels proclaiming its importance, sat upon a marble pedestal. Against this simple backdrop, the bejewelled dagger was a masterpiece.

The dagger gifted by the Swedish ambassador to the Prince Regent was a magnificent example of craftsmanship and regal design, befitting a royal recipient. The hilt of the dagger, crafted from solid gold, had been polished to a high sheen that caught and reflected the candlelight with a warm, inviting glow. Intricately carved into the gold were delicate scrollwork patterns, each curl and flourish meticulously detailed, giving the handle an elegant and opulent appearance.

Embedded within the scrollwork were numerous small, deep red rubies and sparkling diamonds.

Grace hardly noticed the fine steel blade, honed to a dangerous sharpness. Her attention remained near the base of the blade, where she studied the emblem representing the Swedish royal crest. It would forever serve as a nod to the origins of the gift and its significance as a symbol of diplomatic goodwill.

Accustomed though Grace was to luxury and jewels, it was an arresting sight that nearly took her breath away. Even Lady Tilbury was struck dumb by the priceless gift. Only the watchful eyes of the guard standing by the door encouraged them to hurry along.

Grace longed to depart to the quiet of her home, but her night was barely at the beginning. Thanks to the U-shaped layout of the tables, Grace once again had a view of Charity and Roland. They sat near the head of the table, befitting Roland's position as the future Duke of Northumberland. The Tilbury family sat across the way, just above those of the lowest rank. The only pleasure Grace took was from seeing her archenemy, Lady Fitzroy, seated at the foot.

The queen's methods were subtle, but she had found a way to show her dissatisfaction with Lady Fitzroy's role in Charity's kidnapping.

Lady Fitzroy was undaunted. During dinner, more than once Grace overheard her cast mild aspersions on Charity's character. The women around her tittered over her remarks, committing them to memory so that they might share them with others over tea the next day. Grace's cheeks burned with fury, but she bit her tongue.

Her mama's instructions before they left home had been clear. "The best thing you can do for Charity is to pretend as though nothing happened. Soon enough, the ton will forget. You may think to bank the fires of gossip by speaking up on her behalf, but you will only end up fanning the flames instead. Do as the queen has and draw a blanket over the entire matter."

Easier said than done. This was likely why Lady Tilbury made sure to keep Grace distracted with conversation with every eligible gentleman nearby, no matter how ludicrous. Any pairing made here would be a step upward for the Tilbury family. Her mama seemed determined to see Grace make a suitable match before the end of the season, even if only a few weeks remained.

"Lord Sanderson, have you been introduced to my daughter, Lady Grace?" her mama asked of the old man seated across from them at the table. "She has recently made her debut and is strong of spirit. Her future husband will reap fortune through her fortitude."

Between his white hair, age-spotted skin, and hunched shape, Grace marvelled that the man was not yet in the grave. He was certainly old enough to rival Methusaleh and make her reconsider Lord Harrington. Perhaps that was why her mama was so intent on getting the man to pay Grace notice.

Grace gave the man a toothy smile. Given her mother was

*The Ruby Dagger*

describing her as though she were a broodmare, it seemed appropriate. The old lord squinted at her and mumbled something almost unintelligible. She thought he asked something about her hips, but surely the man would not be so gauche. But then he eyed her mother's figure and then studied her anew.

Thank goodness Charity wasn't sitting closer. She would be thrilled to remind Grace of her early-season plan to marry a near-corpse and become a widow.

A footman arrived to clear the last of the dessert plates. With dinner so close to an end, Grace spotted the chance to slip away for some air, before the guests moved on to the post-dinner reception and dancing. She murmured her apologies and asked to be excused. As she left the room, she felt the heat of the old man's gaze burning her behind. What was her mother thinking, to inflict the prospect of marriage to such a man on her?

She stopped a passing footman to ask directions to the nearest courtyard, where she could get some air.

"Follow this hallway, past the throne room, until you are forced to go left. After the turn, you can reach the courtyard through the second door on your right. Would you like me to show you the way?" he offered.

"No, I am certain I can follow your instructions. They are simple enough, and you must be very busy." Grace turned her back on the man to allow him to return to his work. The murmurs of conversation faded as she got farther away from the dining room. The smell of packed bodies, roasted meat, and perfumes was slowly replaced by the melting beeswax of the candles lining the walls.

The courtyard offered little respite from the heated dining room. The air was thick with humidity, with not even a hint of breeze to clear her mind. Nonetheless, Grace meandered around the space, pausing to admire the floral beds in full bloom. She longed to rest on a stone bench, but dared not sit down. Her mama would have her head if anyone noticed her missing overlong.

Grace completed her circuit and returned to the door through which she had exited. She made her way back to the room set aside for the women to refresh themselves. There, she dipped a hand towel in cool water and used it to wipe any hint of sweat from her brow and the back of her neck. Though it made little difference, it was as good as she was going to get.

Thus resigned to return to the event, she swung open the door and stepped outside, expecting the corridor to be empty, and narrowly missed ploughing into someone.

"I am terribly sorry," Grace apologised, while setting herself to rights. "I did not see you."

"Mind on other things?" the other woman asked in a haughty tone.

Grace's head jerked up, and she found herself staring straight into Lady Fitzroy's icy blue eyes.

The woman's smile was as piercing as her gaze. "Perhaps you were thinking about a certain earl? The two of you seemed to be growing close while the diamond was away. Now that she has returned, he cleaves himself to her, leaving you by the wayside."

"We spent our time together searching for Charity," Grace hissed. "As you well know."

"What I know is a far different thing from what others see, Lady Grace. How odd that your family has risen higher, and despite this favour, your own prospects have seen little improvement."

Attempting to look unruffled, Grace straightened her sleeves. "I did not know you cared so much for my prospects, Lady Fitzroy."

Lady Fitzroy's lids flickered slightly. "Any mama would

*The Ruby Dagger*

want to make sure you make the wisest choices. Perhaps you should take care of the company you keep. The diamond has lost some of her lustre, and if you should not mind your path, you may once again find yourself at a crossroads with mine."

With that, Lady Fitzroy lifted her skirt and swished past Grace, sauntering off before Grace could get out a word of reply. Grace balled her hands into fists and gritted her teeth. Were she a man, she could demand satisfaction from the awful woman. Grace did not suffer from blood-thirst, but Lady Fitzroy brought out her basest instincts.

After gulping down air to cool her anger, Grace walked back to the dining room. She lingered around the corner, out of sight of the guests inside, still wrestling with her roiling emotions. She pretended to admire a statue in case anyone else came past.

"Grace?" a familiar male voice called softly. "Are you feeling all right?"

Grace spun around, hardly daring to believe her ears. Lord Roland Percy stood a mere foot away, with his hand outstretched and hanging in the air. A smile nearly lifted the corners of her lips, before her stomach plummeted in shock and fear that someone else would come around the corner. That would be disastrous for everyone—but most especially for her friend.

Cold with nerves, she hissed at him, "What are you *doing* here?"

"I saw you had left... and well, I wanted to check on you."

"Are you mad?" she gasped. She glanced left and right, fearing the echo of footsteps. They could not be found speaking together, not after all her work to convince the ton that there was nothing between them. That he had not been paying calls on her as they thought, but instead asking her for help to find his intended. With Charity returned, there was no reason whatsoever for Grace and Roland to be alone.

"Mad?" he stuttered, confused by her words. "Why—?"

Roland showed no signs of stopping. Grace grabbed his arm and dragged him through the nearest doorway, without giving a second of thought to what room lay on the other side. All that mattered was that it was blessedly empty.

But no sooner had they crossed over the threshold than Roland jerked to a halt. Grace stumbled as his unmoving stiffness pulled her around, off balance, and he reached out to steady her. She turned her head, not wanting to meet his gaze, and that was when she spied the crumpled form of the guard she had last seen in the throne room. His stillness was so unnatural that her mind blared a siren of warning.

The small cry escaped her lips before she could stop it. The view was so shocking; she felt as though lightning had struck her immobile. She couldn't look away, and the longer she stared, the faster her heart raced, making her head spin. It seemed like an eternity, even though it was only seconds, before Roland hauled her around to face away from the corpse.

Whether she had collapsed in towards him, or whether he pulled her into an embrace, she could not be certain. But only with his strong arms around her did she feel safe.

## 2

During dinner, Roland watched Lady Charity eating quietly beside him. The queen's deft handling of Lady Charity's kidnapping—and his subsequent engagement to the girl following the public appearance at church—had cleared much of her tarnished reputation. Still, there were some prudish individuals who whispered doubts loud enough to hear. Not many, but a few. Most accepted the queen's fabricated story, but even amongst these, he saw how many of them watched her like a hawk sizing up a rodent.

He would not give them more reason to doubt her with his behaviour. It gave him a peculiar feeling in the pit of his stomach to feel as though he alone stood between her and defamation. To be so responsible for this... well, near stranger's well being.

As though he could not help it, his gaze slid from Lady Charity to another familiar face sitting on the far end of the U-shaped table. Grace was watching them from where she sat, her lips pressed together. When their gazes clashed, she glanced away, as if embarrassed to be caught staring in his direction.

*No. Look at me,* he thought. But she did not shift her eyes back his way.

Frustrated, Roland turned his head. He had not been able to speak with Grace since they had stood in the queen's chambers two weeks ago. She had been the one to ask for the promise to safeguard Lady Charity. He wished he knew why she now seemed so unhappy about it.

A subtle nudge to his arm caught his attention. On his right side sat Lady Anwen, the Dowager Duchess of Somerset, and he realised he had missed some question she had put to him. "I am sorry, your grace. My mind was a thousand leagues away. What was your question?"

The duchess dimpled at him. "I was wondering, have you set a date yet? Do you expect your engagement will be long or short?"

Lady Charity, overhearing this on his other side, also turned his way. He wondered if she, too, was interested in the answer.

In some respects, it would be a relief to get it over and done with. There was only one answer, however, that wouldn't raise more suspicion about Lady Charity's state. "I see no reason to rush to the altar," he said as rehearsed, trying to summon up graceful words. "Why not spend the long summer days enjoying each other's company? Though—I am happy to bow to my lady's preferences."

"I agree. No need to rush," Lady Charity agreed calmly. "Perhaps a quiet event in the fall when the weather starts to cool, and the leaves begin to turn? Or late summer, before we leave Brighton."

The dowager cooed. "Fall weddings can be lovely. A backdrop of fall leaves will complement your colour wonderfully."

So Roland turned his attention aside once again, deeming his comment successful. The duchess had missed the earlier

*The Ruby Dagger*

excitement of the season so far, but her prattling bid fair to make up for it in the shortest possible amount of time. She filled the gaps caused by the quietness of her nearby tablemates in spades. His only relief was that at least she seemed to be one of the ones inclined to be kind to Lady Charity.

Footmen had only just finished serving the final course—a pineapple cream flavoured with cardamom and served in glittering crystal bowls. As everyone around him seemed to enjoy it, he put a spoonful of the rich dessert in his mouth. Roland's gaze wandered once more to the far arm of the table without his conscious thought. That was when he noticed that, at some point, Lady Grace had left it. The tart cream in his mouth turned sour.

Several minutes later, people spoke of the coming reception, and Grace had still not returned. His nerves demanded he stay at this interminable dinner no longer. He left Lady Charity sitting at the table with a brief comment that he would find her at the reception.

The relative coolness of the hallway felt like a slap in the face compared to the heat of the cloistered dining room they had been sitting in, and Roland took a moment just to breathe. Where had Grace gone? Had she gone to one of the many private refreshment rooms made available to the guests? He headed in that direction, hoping that perhaps they would cross paths, and hoping he could find a moment to finally speak with her.

Luck, it seemed, was finally on his side.

Lady Grace was dawdling in the hallway near these rooms, just around the corner from the attentive footmen who waited to serve guests needing a moment of privacy. She was pretending to admire some statue, but he knew better.

"Grace?" he called softly, not wanting to startle her. "Are you feeling all right?"

She spun with such alacrity that he stepped backwards in surprise. "What are you doing here?" she hissed at him.

Had he said something foolish in showing concern for her wellbeing? She had the audacity to grab him by the wrist and pull him out of the hallway. Into another room, where they would be out of view of a casual glance.

The doorway seemed familiar. There should have been a guard at this door, he realised, for it was the throne room. The expensive gift from the Swedes had been left on display for the pleasure of the exclusive invitation list. It took a moment for him to acknowledge that a sudden disquiet had stirred in his gut. Something was amiss.

Instinct made Roland stop short, causing Grace to stumble, and he grabbed her arms to steady her. There—that's when they both saw it: the guard's body crumpled just steps away.

A small sound of distress escaped her lips, and Roland curled his arms around her, turning her away from the view. Briefly, she buried her face in his shoulder, but then she almost wrenched herself away, and she stared at him, eyes wide, her face ashen.

"Divert your eyes from him—focus on me," he said, speaking softly as he maintained his grasp on her arms, worried that she might faint. "Grace. It is all right."

She let loose a strangled laugh. "All right? He... he..." unable to say more, she brought shaking hands to her mouth.

"It is all right," he repeated. "Whoever did this... they are gone."

She moaned, and then she struggled to get her emotions under control. "I—I've never seen someone dead. Not... not like this," she added hastily. "The maid... she looked perhaps only like she had fallen asleep on the floor."

He could well imagine. The maid had fallen over the bannister, and Grace had seen a glimpse only from the upper

*The Ruby Dagger*

floor. In any event, a death by such misadventure was a far cry from seeing a guard with a hunting knife protruding from between his ribs and bloody froth upon his lips.

Unable to help himself, he set his hand to her cheek. "I need to inform someone. Will you be all right? Just for a moment? I will not go far. Just around the corner to find the footman by the refreshment rooms."

Grace nodded tightly, keeping her eyes on his.

"Good. Remember to breathe and do not look. I will be right back; I promise."

Roland strode out at a pace just short of a run, waving at the footman for the servant's attention even as he turned the corner. With alacrity, the royal servant met Roland partway. After hearing the grim news, the footman left his post to go seek the queen forthwith.

It was only a minute, perhaps two, that he had been gone, but he was afraid he would return to find Grace collapsed on the floor as well. Fortunately, though distressed, she seemed to have collected herself in his absence. She had even turned to make an assessment of the dead guard, though she kept her distance from him.

"You should not be looking," he chastised her. "This is no sight for a lady."

"I am all right, Lord Percy," she murmured, looking up at him. "It was just the shock of finding him this way."

Something in his guts twisted at the way she had returned to stiff formality with him. "Can you find your way back to the reception unescorted? I will deal with this. Go to your mama and Lady Charity."

She gave him a measured glance that he could not interpret. "And will you deal with this by investigating the cause?"

Taken aback, he paused. "I had no desire or thought to do such a thing, but I must serve the queen's whim, I suppose. I would think with so many military men in attendance, she will likely have no need for the likes of me."

"You should not belittle your skills in that manner," she said, crossing her arms over her stomach. But she turned away again.

Confused, Roland decided that at least for the moment Grace was all right, and he turned to examine the body a little more closely—or at least as closely as he could without touching anything. The hunting knife's steel was buried to the hilt in flesh, and its handle was wrapped serviceably in leather. The frayed edge revealed the shiny gold band that capped off the butt of the handle. If it had any marks to identify the maker or owner, they would not be discerned until it was pulled free.

Roland would not do so while Grace was nearby. There was a limit to how much he was willing to test her mettle.

"Do you think Lady Fitzroy could have done this?" Grace asked him.

His eyebrows raised high on his forehead. "Do I think Lady Fitzroy could overcome a grown man and a guard, no less? I do not think so. I do not believe any lady could have driven the blade home in such a manner? Why do you ask?"

"I saw her. In the hall," Grace said contemplatively. "Before you found me."

Blinking, Roland considered it once more, but he finally shook his head. "It would be easy with our experiences to... to imagine her as the villain. Still, we cannot jump to such a conclusion or overlook the physical strength of the feat. And... why? Why would she do such a thing?" Roland straightened up looking around the empty throne room. "Why, for that matter, would anyone else murder the guard?"

The queen's icy voice pulled him around. "Perhaps one would do it to cover the theft of the ambassador's gift," she said.

# 3

Grace followed the direction of the queen's outstretched arm, her gaze landing upon the ivory cushion. There was no sign of the magnificent ruby encrusted dagger that had laid upon it earlier.

"I would ask you to turn out your pockets, but given the fact that you sent for me, I am assuming neither of you is responsible." Queen Charlotte's scowl deepened. "Are you two making a habit of turning up anytime something terrible happens? Why were you in this room? *Together?*"

Grace's eyes widened. Fear clamped her throat, her mouth as barren as a desert. She had not wanted anyone to see her and Roland together. Now the queen was asking questions for which she had no ready answer.

Roland came through with a reply. "I bumped into Lady Grace in the corridor and stopped to say good evening. I noticed the absence of the guard and opened the door to make sure all was well. That was when we made our discovery."

It was a small lie, but a lie nonetheless. Grace closed her eyes once briefly, grateful for his discretion.

The queen sniffed, making it clear she did not fully believe his answer. As always, Queen Charlotte was nobody's fool, much less theirs. But rather than call Roland upon it, she allowed the conversation to move onto more important matters. "Do you mean to say that someone has dared to come into my home, kill my guard, and steal a gift of state? While we were all making merry just down the corridor?"

"So it would seem, Your Majesty." Roland held his hands wide. "Given the staff in the corridors, I cannot imagine how someone infiltrated this far into the palace without the right to be here."

"Then it could be a guest, which makes the insult even worse. There is a viper nestling against my bosom and I mean to have their head," the queen demanded. "Lady Grace, you left earlier than Lord Percy. Did you see anyone come by? Do not play reticent with me. I have already had a demonstration of your acute eye for the unusual."

"I stepped into a nearby courtyard to get some air, following the directions of a footman. I was not outside long, but certainly someone could have passed along the hall during that window of time without me seeing. The only person I encountered upon my return was Lady Fitzroy." Grace stopped short, but her mind continued to play through the possibilities. "The countess has proved herself willing to risk angering the crown. Perhaps she is taking the society games to another level."

"Lady Fitzroy is daring, but surely she is not fool enough to take such an obvious swipe at me."

Grace's forehead wrinkled. "She got away with her previous misbehaviour. Perhaps she has become emboldened."

"Is that what you think?" Queen Charlotte arched one imperious eyebrow and scowled at Grace. "It seems you have not noticed then that Lady Fitzroy has found many doors closed to her of late. The only reason she is here tonight is because she is an acquaintance of the ambassador. Did you not note her

*The Ruby Dagger*

seating arrangement? I sat her at the foot of the table, far below where her title would afford her a chair."

"So Lady Charity noted as we were heading to dinner," Roland said. When the queen looked his way, he added, "She is sensitive to the undercurrents of the ton, ma'am."

"Clearly," the queen replied, glancing between the two young people. "Moving forward, Lord Percy, I suggest you delegate any plans with regard to checking on someone to my diamond rather than acting on impetus. You seem to struggle with the simple task of maintaining propriety."

Grace kept her gaze firmly fixed on the floor, not wanting to do anything to raise the queen's ire any further.

Roland bowed his head in resignation. "I will follow your advice, my queen."

"See that you do. Now, there remains the issue at hand—identifying the thief and recovering the gift in haste so its loss does not have to be mentioned to Ambassador Lindberg. How will you proceed?"

Surprised, Roland looked back up. "Are you certain we are the wisest choice—?"

The queen fixed him with a look, and he fell silent. "Yes, you. You are already aware of the theft, and the fewer involved tonight, the better."

This was a much more delicate matter than searching for a girl everyone knew had been missing, and Roland paused, considering how this tied his hands. "Should we send for Lady Fitzroy to ask her what she might have seen?" At his side, Grace elbowed him slightly, which he took to mean definitely not. "Or send for Bow Street?" Roland ventured again.

"Here? Those ruffians?" The queen's expression soured. "They will run riot through the halls, with no respect for the fine furnishings. And they lack discretion. I wish to keep the incident as quiet as possible, not inform every resident of London.."

Grace dared to speak up, mostly to keep Roland from further irritating the queen with improper suggestions. "How should we go about checking if it might have been a servant, Your Majesty?"

Queen Charlotte stiffened. "It is difficult to credit the possibility. Only a very clever thief, certain of his ability to get away with it, would dare. Or a very stupid one. Because a servant stealing an object of such value would, at the very best, be on the next transport to the penal colony. At worst, I would have a word with the magistrate to ensure he would swing."

Finally, the queen shook her head. "There is no higher honour for one of the servant class than to serve here in the palace. They are compensated well enough, and loyal, because they know any hint of lesser misbehaviours would result in them being cast out without references. They would never work in an English household again. This line of thought is foolish. I have fifty guests waiting for me to reappear. I do not want a single hint of this incident reaching the ears of the ton tonight."

Grace could recognise the wisdom of the queen's statement, harsh as it was. With a mad king locked away and his son ruling in his stead, the crown had already suffered much damage and she would be eager to keep this quiet.

Roland, however, failed to follow her logic. "Ma'am, if I may be so bold. We could bring this matter to a quick close by simply searching—"

"Heavens!" Grace cried out, desperately wanting to prevent Roland from finishing that statement. "Searching their persons would be an insult of the highest level."

The queen flashed Grace a cunning smile. "Some of my diamond's wit has rubbed off on you, at least."

*The Ruby Dagger*

Grace bobbed a curtsy at the compliment, biting though it was.

"I can have someone see to the servants after the event's end, for they will be in no rush to depart. With regard to everyone else, the situation calls for subtlety. The first order of business is to retrieve that jewelled dagger, lest this become a diplomatic issue."

"You fear the Swedes would view the loss of their token of friendship as a sign of lack of appreciation on our part," Grace murmured, wringing her hands.

Queen Charlotte nodded. "Indeed. Now you understand why this matter must be handled with kid gloves. We are not discussing the reputation of a single young lady, but the possibility of a diplomatic break between two nations."

The seriousness of the matter took Grace's breath away. To think, while she had walked past, someone had been inside this very room, stabbing a guard and making away with a priceless gift. If she had stepped away from the dinner earlier, or returned inside a moment sooner, maybe she would have seen the villain leaving the room.

Or maybe she had.

Despite the queen's statements, Grace could not let go of the possibility that Lady Fitzroy was somehow involved.

The queen raised her hand again, this time pointing her finger at Roland. "You will find out who did this and deliver them to me, with all haste. News of this will slip from the walls for certain. It is only a matter of when. A day of silence is all I can guarantee before the murder is known about. No more."

Roland swallowed. "I am not an experienced investigator, ma'am. I am a soldier by training, better suited for holding a weapon in the firing line once the guilty are identified."

"And yet, you found my diamond."

"We found your diamond," Grace said, surprising even

herself. "I mean, that is, to say that I helped. And I can do so again, with your permission, ma'am."

The queen raised her finger to tap it against her chin. The gemstones on the rings on her fingers sparkled in the candle-lit chandelier. "Why? Last time, the desire to see your dearest friend restored drove you onwards. How can I trust you will not drop the matter at the first hint of trouble?"

Roland frowned at Grace, his expression begging her to hold her tongue, or to somehow take back the words she had said. Doubtless, he wanted her to stay safe in the box in which society placed her. An unmarried woman with little prospects, her only value coming from the dowry her father would provide.

These last two weeks had proven how impossible it was for Grace to accept that as her future. Every mindless conversation about the weather or who was seen together chafed at her will to continue with the season.

She missed her conversations with Roland and his openness to her opinions. Though he was engaged to Charity, there remained the possibility that he could become her friend. They could remain in contact, working together to put things like this to rights. He would understand this eventually.

Grace was willing to grasp onto any lifeline, even one as tenuous as this.

She took a deep breath and ploughed ahead. "I have already encountered the first trouble. I had every chance to turn tail and run when we discovered your guard's body. There would be no way for anyone to know I was in this room with Lord Percy. But I stayed, Your Majesty. I stood still and answered your pointed questions. I remained and still do, ready to serve the crown however it is needed. You said you need someone subtle. Well, who would guess I am involved? The fact that everyone dismisses me out of hand is my greatest value. I can do this. You simply need to grant me permission."

*The Ruby Dagger*

"Grace! No," Roland cautioned, forgetting to use her formal address in his upset. "We are talking about a murderer."

Grace gritted her teeth and faced his fury head on. "I know. The body of this brave man still lies in this room. I cannot forget."

"Your reputation," he said, trying again. "What if Lady Fitzroy *is* involved? She is aware of your penchant for sticking your nose in."

"I will be careful."

"You are being foolish."

"Enough!" the queen demanded, interrupting the pair. She raised a hand to stave off anything else Roland wanted to say. "During your court presentation, Lady Grace, I judged you as impertinent. I made an error in seeing that as a black mark against you. You speak up when you should remain mum. Stick your nose where it is not welcome. I can either ban you from the palace or count this as a strength within my fold. Despite Lord Percy's arguments, I am of the mind to do the latter."

Grace's vision swam as she listened to the queen. She must have misheard, for it seemed the queen was saying yes.

"Then there is no other choice for it," Roland said in a heavy tone.

"Excellent!" the queen clapped her hands together and rubbed them in satisfaction. "You two have an established way of working. I shall leave you to it. I have been absent overlong as it is."

Grace did not bother to hide the smile from her face as she turned to face Roland. "Where do you want to start?"

Roland's shoulders dropped into a defeated slump. He wiped a hand over his face and cast a glance at the body still laying on the floor. "Return to the reception with the queen. We need people in the room to detect if anyone is behaving suspiciously. I trust you to parse that out."

Grace nodded in agreement. "What of the servants?"

"I will send someone to assist with them," Queen Charlotte said. "Even if they are not involved in the theft, they will be aware of which guests absented themselves from the table. They always are," she added, leaving Grace with the suspicion that the queen often took advantage of this source of information.

"With your approval, I will send for my man to assist me with gathering evidence here. I trust him with my life and all secrets."

The queen waved her hand. "Do as you see fit, so long as you keep this quiet. Come, Lady Grace. Your reputation can gain a helping hand from walking into the room behind me."

# 4

Roland dispatched the footman post-haste to find his valet and then turned his attention to the dead man. He had seen many forms of death over the years of war, but that did not mean he was at all comfortable with it.

He steeled himself for the task at hand and approached the body where it lay. The guard's bright red coat vividly stood out against the wooden floor, shining with its gleaming brass buttons and white piping. The coat's long tails wrinkled slightly under his fallen form. Based on the man's silver epaulettes, he judged him to be a lieutenant. Not a newcomer then. And yet, he had fallen without much of a fight.

To judge by the guard's face, stricken with pain and fear even in death, and the blood trickling from the corners of his mouth, it had not been a swift death. Nevertheless, it likely was a silent one. Based on the placement of the handle, the death blow had been made deliberately low, through the lung instead of the heart. As the lung collapsed and the chest filled with blood, the man would have been unable to cry out. Unable to take a breath to raise an alarm. He spent his last long moments drowning in his own blood, with nothing to do but contemplate the manner of his demise.

He had seen men die this way before. It was a terrible way to go.

The sound of footsteps entering the room tugged Roland's attention from the body, and he looked up to see Thorne striding swiftly towards him. More than ten years ago, Thorne had left Northumberland with Roland to serve as his batman, and so he too had the experience of the battlefield to guide him. Roland made him his valet after being recalled by the duke, glad for the man's continued presence at his side.

Thorne cast a thorough glance at the scene and settled back on his heels, expecting him to provide an explanation.

"It seems someone was willing to kill the guard in order to steal the ruby dagger being displayed here," Roland told him. "The queen is, of course, furious, and has put me to the task."

"I see," Thorne said, crouching lower so that he could better study the scene.

"Everyone was here prior to the dinner, and Grace and I were here shortly after the conclusion of it," Roland added, pitching his voice lower so it would not echo in the vast room. Thorne gave him a sidelong glance at Grace's name, but he ignored it. "So, the murder occurred during that time."

Removing his gloves, Thorne gently reached out to touch the side of the guard's face. "He is still quite warm, so that seems to follow."

Roland nodded, mostly to himself. While he was not a physician or a surgeon, most military men of any experience had at least a passing familiarity with the mechanics of death. Once a person's spirit had fled, that which stoked the inner fires was extinguished, and the body would gradually lose its warmth. The dinner had stretched for nearly four hours, and if the skin had not noticeably cooled, then it would also follow that the killer had most likely not taken the liberty of committing this crime at the very start of the meal.

"If I have been sent to you, and through closed doors, I trust the queen is not interested in letting the news spread," Thorne deduced. "But you and I are also not investigators. How can I assist?"

Roland rubbed his jaw, thinking. "Because of the range of suspects involved, the queen has tasked me with checking the members of the ton who were invited tonight. I need you to act as an intermediary and gather some of this information from the queen's servants."

"Who was present?" Thorne guessed, his blue eyes turning speculative. "And who left the tables?"

"Yes. The master of ceremonies would likely have the former. The latter... you might have to ask some of the servants who are in the room. Hopefully, the queen has had a discreet word with the butler that you are to be given all cooperation."

Thorne nodded and got to his feet, smoothing his breeches down. "Then I will begin immediately."

After Thorne left, Roland considered the body longer, and then looked around the room. He recalled that the guard had been stationed outside of the throne room's doors. In death, he lay some three paces inside of it. Since the poor man's death had not been quick, it stood to some reason that he might have had a period of lucidity in which he would have instinctively sought help. The nearest place to seek help, however, would be situated outside the room.

Perhaps he had attempted to follow his murderer into the room. To stop him. He could believe that of a career guard of this man's age... except.

The way he lay, mostly straight-limbed, was at odds with the manner of a man who was either drowning in blood or attempting one final heroic act. Looking closer at the lay of the man's uniform, Roland would wager that he had been dragged out of sight at least some of the distance. Perhaps the man had never left his post at all. At least, not while he had been alive. But if that were the case... if the man had been stabbed in the hallway and brought inside, the dead weight of the guard would likely have been far too considerable for a lady.

Grace would be unhappy to find there was more evidence disproving Lady Fitzroy's involvement, but facts were facts.

The crack of the door opening brought Roland upright again, wondering who was interrupting now. Thorne again already? But no—the man who stepped through was wearing the formal blue dress uniform of the military, and immediately all the thoughts of investigating murder fled from his mind.

The man was older than Roland remembered, some fifty years now. His chestnut hair had developed into brilliant silver streaks at the temples, but Roland would still recognise this man anywhere by his posture alone.

"Colonel Green?" Roland exclaimed, striding forward to greet him. "It has been far too long."

"Clearly," the man replied, his washed out blue eyes twinkling with good humour and no censure. "I have been going by Sir David for some time now, Roland. Or should I call you Earl Percy now?"

Unable to help himself, Roland's smile stretched fit to crack his face. "Please, sir, Roland is fine. How are you? How have you been? I saw you earlier at the presentation, but we were too far apart. I was going to seek you out at the reception."

"Retired now, sadly, but still keeping quite busy. It seems you appear to be as well. But let me get a look at you," Sir David said, grabbing a hold of Roland's shoulders and looking him over. "You have grown into quite the strapping man. Much better than that green young colt I remember who joined my

*The Ruby Dagger*

regiment ten years ago. Did you stay with the cavalry? Has it truly been so long?"

"Time has flown," Roland agreed. "Yes, I stayed with the cavalry until I was recalled after my father's death."

Sir David let him go, nodding sagely, not expressing his condolences for Thaddius' death at all. David knew precisely how Roland felt about his father. "For what it is worth, my lad, the service appears to have stood you in good stead. I hope they miss you."

Roland waved a dismissal of that. He doubted the cavalry missed him as much as they did Sir David, for the man had been a powerful force to be reckoned with and a good commander. Few young officers could experience a better one. "It is possible that they may have me back in a year or so again, once I have secured the line with an heir. So if they do miss me, they should not want for it very long."

"Yes. I did hear that you caused quite the rumpus with your bride-to-be," Sir David smiled. "Lady Charity is a pretty thing. You might not want to go back."

Roland's chest tightened uncomfortably at the thought of being married and staying in London, bearing a couple of heirs and then attending balls and events until he passed of old age—or perhaps boredom. Noncommittally, he shrugged. "We shall see. But never mind all that," he deftly changed the subject. "Why are you here?"

"Ah. Well, that is easily explained! I served for two years as Commander-in-Chief during the period of Prince Frederick's... regrettable situation." Sir David's brows drew down. "Despite the brevity, it gave me some useful experience of overseeing the palace guard and staff. The queen approached me when she returned to the reception. I will be conducting the search and interrogation of the servants, but the queen also asked that I aid you however I might. I am at your service."

"My, the tables have truly turned." Roland smiled. "You might cross paths with Thorne then, as I sent Thorne to gather a list of who got up from the table. He may require your aid more than I."

Sir David laughed and clapped Roland on the shoulder. "Your batman! I recall young Thorne. A good lad, too. Always polite and clever, that one. He is still in your service then? Good, good. I shall look forward to renewing our acquaintance. Keep him close; a servant of such excellent character is worth his weight in gold."

"Always, Sir David," Roland agreed truthfully. "I do not know what I would do without him. I am sure he will remember you as fondly as I do."

"Do not harbour any concerns. I will make sure the servants cooperate with him if he is also assisting you with this... disastrous mess." Sir David looked down at the body, scowling in disgust. "And for that matter, if you have looked your fill at it, I will also send someone to clean... that up."

Roland looked down at the body. He had only given the murder weapon the most cursory of examinations. "I have not been able to find an identifying mark on the hunting knife, but I dare not take the blade out, especially if I am to go back to the reception," he admitted.

"Of course, lad. You need to return to the reception before people suspect something untoward or amiss. Leave the messy work to someone else," Sir David said, cocking his head at the corpse. "There may be some maker's mark on the handle beneath the wrapped leather, or perhaps engraved on the flat of the blade or ricasso. It is easily done. I will look for a mark when we remove it."

"Thank you. I cannot begin to imagine how returning to the party spotted with blood would cause my reputation to suffer.

*The Ruby Dagger*

Or Lady Charity's." Roland said sourly. "She stands perhaps more to lose from my actions than I."

Sir David nodded knowingly, but gave Roland a wink. "Do not undervalue your own worth in the bargain, *Lord Percy*. You are the heir to a dukedom and there is a blushing young debutante waiting to be your bride. Go back to her. Raise a glass, enjoy the companionship of the highest of gentlemen and ladies, and bask in the queen's favour. These things are too important to treat so casually."

Lady Charity's virtue had to be protected, but he still did not want to ape the manners of a courtly gentleman for the ton. But Sir David was right; some things he should not treat casually... such as his plans for the wedding and honeymoon, as Thorne had suggested only days past. Abruptly, Roland was annoyed. As obnoxious as it was to go to balls and events, he preferred to be annoyed at that inconvenience than to face the idea of marriage and everything that came after.

Nevertheless, needs must. He bowed slightly to Sir David and headed back to the reception. But first, he went by way of the refreshment rooms to ensure that his appearance was still acceptable.

# 5

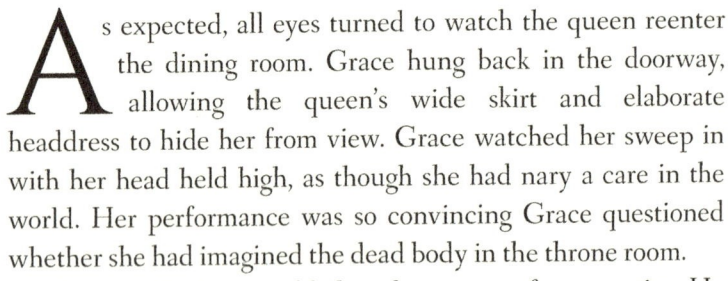

As expected, all eyes turned to watch the queen reenter the dining room. Grace hung back in the doorway, allowing the queen's wide skirt and elaborate headdress to hide her from view. Grace watched her sweep in with her head held high, as though she had nary a care in the world. Her performance was so convincing Grace questioned whether she had imagined the dead body in the throne room.

Queen Charlotte nodded at the master of ceremonies. He clapped his hands twice to get everyone's attention. "Ladies and gentlemen, I have the distinct honour of inviting you to adjourn to the Cornwall Chamber, where we shall indulge in the finest selections of drink, complemented by an exquisite assortment of cheeses and the season's choicest fruits. Please, allow yourselves to be guided by the light of camaraderie and the anticipation of continued delightful conversation."

As one, the guests rose from the table and moved into a line, following the queen as she led the way into the next room. Grace waited until the highest ranking guests had gone before slipping into the dining room. If she thought to avoid notice, she was mistaken.

*The Ruby Dagger*

Her mother locked arms with her and tugged her close. "Where have you been?" she whispered. "And more importantly, have you angered our queen?"

"No, Mama," Grace reassured her. "There is naught to cause you concern. I will explain later."

Lady Tilbury cast a sideways glance at her youngest child and searched her face for any hint of a lie. Grace's smile was firmly fixed. Grace allowed her mother to guide her toward the doorway to the Cornwall Room. She stiffened when the queen turned their way.

Queen Charlotte raised an eyebrow at Grace, issuing a silent order to stop talking to her mama and to get to work finding the missing diplomatic gift.

Grace slipped free of her mother, explaining she wanted to pay her regards to Charity. Lady Tilbury nodded her head in agreement, but gave a final word of warning. "Our queen's favour shifts faster than the wind. See you stay clear of the cold edge."

After availing herself of a glass of sherry from a passing server, Grace meandered her way around the room. The older and the more inebriated members of the ton relaxed upon silk and velvet covered settees. Platters of cheeses of all varieties, sugared fruit, and ripe summer berries sat on tables. The deep red strawberries turned Grace's stomach, reminding her at once of both the missing ruby dagger and the red coat of the murdered guard. She held tight to the stem of her glass and remembered why she was there.

Charity stood on the opposite side of the room, facing Grace but not looking her way. She had her attention fixed on the men standing before her. Grace did not pay the men too much attention. Men always lined up to speak with Charity, but now that she was engaged, the conversations tended to be brief. Grace suspected that men stopped only long enough to test her friend's commitment to her forthcoming marriage. As soon as they understood she was indeed off the market, they moved on.

Grace intended to wait for the conversation to end, but Charity noticed her approach and motioned for her to join in. She slid over to make room for Grace to stand beside her. "Gentlemen, may I introduce my dearest friend, Lady Grace Tilbury? Lady Grace, our regent requires no introduction, but mayhap you have not yet met his honoured guest, Baron Gustaf Albin Lindberg."

Grace shifted her wine glass into her left hand and swept into a curtsy as appropriate for greeting the Prince Regent. She held the pose long enough to convey respect and then rose to address the men. "It is my honour to speak with you, Your Highness, and to make your acquaintance, Baron Lindberg."

Grace expected the prince to nod his head in acknowledgement and then hasten to introduce the visiting ambassador to more important guests. To her horror, he stayed put. He must have heard something of her efforts to find Charity when she was kidnapped. That was the only explanation Grace could find for why he showed any interest in her.

While her mother was likely swooning in delight at seeing her daughter converse with the highest ranking men in the room, Grace was deeply uncomfortable. The queen expected her to watch for signs of unusual behaviour, and certainly did not count her son or the ambassador among the pool of suspects. God save Grace should the queen glance her way and misinterpret the moment. If she thought Grace likely to mention anything about the murder and theft, she would call for her head on the spot.

Yet, she could hardly run away. If nothing else, Grace reasoned, she was well positioned to catch sight of any cross looks aimed at Prinny or the ambassador. Prinny swiped a bite

*The Ruby Dagger*

of cheese from a nearby tray and popped it into his mouth. This was, by far and away, the closest Grace had ever been to the man, and she could not help but study him.

The Prince Regent presented an imposing figure, his countenance marked by a life of indulgence and opulence. His visage bore the weight of his years and his responsibilities, with his hair, though receding, carefully arranged and powdered, a nod to an earlier fashion he seemed loath to abandon. His attire was of the finest cut. Despite the corpulence that tales of his banquets had led her to anticipate, his bearing was dignified, his presence commanding the room with an air of undeniable authority and charisma. The royal regalia and the opulent jewels he wore spoke volumes of his love for luxury and display. Yet, it was his eyes, keen and observant, that suggested a mind as sharply dressed as his person.

"Well met, Lady Grace. How are you finding this evening?" Prinny asked.

"Beyond my wildest imaginings, Your Highness," Grace answered honestly. "I never dreamed of attending such an event."

"You are one of Lord Tilbury's progeny?" He did not wait for a response before turning to the ambassador. "Lindberg, you must extend your stay long enough to venture out to our countryside. I am sure Marlborough would be happy to host you at Blenheim so that you can take in the Cotswold hills which Lady Grace's family calls home. Are they not lovely, Lady Grace?"

"They are, indeed, especially now, while the canola is in their final bloom. From our home, the verdant green fields are interspersed with such shades of yellow that they appear like drops of pure sunshine upon a green quilt," she agreed.

Charity gave Grace a sharp glance in surprise at Grace's

poetic response. Grace smiled innocently, giving no hint that she had read that description in a book years before.

"As much as it would be a pleasure to visit the country, I cannot extend my stay. I am expected to return post haste, for my movements are at the pleasure of our monarch. Such is the life of an ambassador."

"What if *I* order you to remain awhile?" Prinny asked, his gaze sharpening. "You are here at my pleasure as much as at Carl Johan's."

The ambassador smiled slightly, dancing around the question. "It is an honour for the company of one such as myself to be in such high demand. But one must ask, would your interest remain if my loyalty could be swayed from my own kingdom so easily? I must serve my monarch's requests to the best of my abilities, just as you would expect me to if I were your ambassador, Your Highness. It is with regret that I must take my leave earlier than either of us might like."

Prinny's brows furrowed, but he could find no fault with the ambassador's reply. Still, he was not ready to retract his claws. He clapped the man on his shoulder. "Come, Lindberg, and allow me to tempt you with more of England's charms. Enjoy yourselves, my ladies," he added in closing to Grace and Charity before steering the ambassador away.

Grace's legs shook, and she grabbed hold of Charity with her free hand lest she stumble. Ever the dedicated friend, Charity patted Grace on the arm. "Come now, Grace, you acquitted yourself well. There is no need to suffer from an attack of the vapours simply because you exchanged words with our future sovereign."

"How I do wish that was all that concerned me," Grace muttered under her breath. "Come, we must have a word."

Grace pulled Charity toward a small alcove she had noticed near the window. In her efforts to avoid embarrassing herself on the dance floor at balls, she availed of such locations often enough to have an eye for where to find them. Fortunately, although a harpist strummed a faint melody to entertain the guests, there was no risk of being asked to dance. Grace needed privacy for a more important reason.

Charity allowed Grace to lead her, paying little attention to their destination. She was searching the room for any sign of her betrothed. "Grace, did you see Lord Percy while you were out of the dining room?"

Grace waited to reply until they were out of earshot of most guests. "Yes, but... There has been a murder," she whispered.

Charity turned a deadly shade of pale. Finally, she gasped, "Lord Percy?"

"No, he is fine," Grace said quickly, realising her lack of adroitness caused Charity to misunderstand. "He remained behind to oversee the body."

Charity's fearful expression relaxed, but now she looked confused. "Instead of returning to the event? Why? Are you certain he is all right?"

"I promise, he is fine, Charity. He sent for the queen, and she instructed us to look into the matter."

"Us?" Charity's eyebrows were practically in her hairline. "You were together with Lord Percy and the queen? With a body? Grace, what on earth is going on?"

Charity's questions tumbled out faster than Grace could reply. The situation was made worse by Grace's inability to fire off answers, for she had not given any thought to how Charity might view the situation. Under any other circumstances, Charity's opinion would be of utmost importance. Grace had been so caught up on finding the dead man, convincing the queen to let her investigate, and then the distraction with the crown prince, all else had faded from her mind.

"I think perhaps I had better start at the beginning," Grace confessed, and by Charity's expression, it was clear she agreed. There was no choice for it but to carry on with the half truth Roland had told the queen. She explained why she had got up from the table and gone for a walk.

"Lord Percy happened upon me and was taking me to sit down. That is when we stumbled across the body." Grace waved her hand in a 'so there you have it' gesture. "From there, other priorities took over. At any rate, that was not the most important thing I have to tell you. You will not believe who else I saw wandering the halls!"

Charity blinked at the torrent of information, tossed about like a sailor on deck during a gale.

"Lady Fitzroy," Grace said, not wanting to wait for Charity to catch up. She wiggled her eyebrows to emphasise her point.

Unfortunately, Charity was not concerned with this bit of news for the same reason. "Did she see you? With Lord Percy?"

"What?" Grace blurted again. "No, I bumped into her a few minutes earlier. But do you see? She was off on her own at the time a guard was killed."

"You think she saw something?" Charity's brows drew together. "Tread very carefully, Grace."

"I suspect more than that. She is involved in the guard's stabbing. I know it."

A shiver shook Charity's shoulders. "Thinking and having unquestionable proof are two very different matters. Given you and the queen are both here, pretending all is well, I presume you lack a witness who can place the weapon in her hand. I cannot even begin to imagine why you believe she would do such a thing. Leave it be, Grace."

And with those words, Grace grasped that Charity must know the whole of it—about the ambassador's gift having gone missing. Until she knew, of course, she would not understand why Grace would suspect Lady Fitzroy. Despite the queen's

*The Ruby Dagger*

concerns, Charity would be the soul of discretion and could be trusted to know. But now was not the time or place to discuss it. Not here, where the walls may have ears.

Grace reached out and took Charity's hands. "There is more, much more, but I cannot speak of it here. I will find you tomorrow. Will you be at home?"

"Yes, we are expecting callers. Come early, so that we might find a moment of privacy. But Grace," Charity added, "when you said the queen instructed you to look into the matter, you mean for tonight, right?"

Grace felt a swell of pride at her friend's question, because for the first time, she was able to share news of her own. "Much better than that. I impressed her with my dedicated search for you, and she has given her approval for us to take the lead on this most sensitive matter. A death in the palace can hardly be trusted to the runners."

Charity bit her lip and glanced aside. "No, I suppose not. But on your own?"

"No, with Lord Percy," Grace hastened to add. "We shall work in tandem, as we did before. You will see, for I will explain everything. But not here and not now. Tomorrow!"

Grace squeezed Charity's hands before pulling free. She had a task to undertake, and she intended to study everyone's behaviour until it was time to depart. And so, she turned her back on her friend, and stalked off without a backwards glance.

# 6

The scrape of his door opening woke Roland from slumber. He whipped his head around to see who was bothering him at this ungodly hour and immediately regretted it. It was only Thorne, but Roland briefly considered chucking one of the fancy, down-stuffed linen pillows at him, anyway.

Upon returning to the reception, he had joined some of the gentlemen for stronger spirits than was his wont. Not only had it given him the opportunity to mingle among the men, keeping an ear to the ground for a guilty party, the liquor helped to settle unsettled nerves. A murder and a theft at the palace during such a lavish event was unprecedented. No wonder the queen was so motivated to keep it from being faffed about.

Roland could count the number of times he had been foxed in his life on one hand—the first night he had returned to London being the last of them. He did not care for the results that came from overindulging. Despite the fact that he hadn't consumed more than a few drinks, the whisky he so seldom drank decided not to sit well on top of the rich dinner, nonetheless.

*The Ruby Dagger*

Or perhaps there were other things last night that had made him unwell.

"Too early. Go away," he instructed Thorne after his stomach ceased its attempts to evacuate.

"What? And waste Mrs Archer's excellent breakfast?" Thorne teased him.

Roland made a sound and pulled the pillow over his head instead.

"They will not eat until we do," Thorne reminded him, and that was what forced him to navigate his way upright in the end.

On the heels of his engagement to Lady Charity, Thorne had informed him in no uncertain terms that it was past time to hire staff. He left the matter in Thorne's hands, and after just a few days, Thorne had found the perfect pair.

Albert Archer was an old veteran of the American Rebellion and former batman himself. He had served his previous master, Sir Harold Grimsby, faithfully until the man's death. Sir Harold's idiot son, having ascended to the title, was embarrassed to keep a butler who walked with a slight limp as a souvenir of his years of service. The new Lord Grimsby was more than happy to allow him to be hired away. His loss.

Eleanor, Albert's wife, came with him, and promptly took to overseeing virtually every domestic chore normally run by maids and housekeeper. It was easy to handle all the washing, sewing and cooking when it was just the four adults and the kids, she had commented.

Eleanor Archer had worked magic on the two orphan children he had found hiding in Fitzroy's townhouse, and for that alone, Roland was pleased by her presence. Willa—the young girl who had been hiding in the stables under the guise of 'Will'—had felt safe enough to emerge from her disguise. She even agreed to spend some time indoors, assisting with cleaning the house from top to bottom just two short days after Mrs Archer's arrival.

Given the small size of the household staff, Roland and Thorne did what they could to assist. In fact, they informed her that they had cleaned up the house when they had arrived. But she had checked the mantles, insisted a *man* couldn't clean anything anyhow, and shooed them off.

Their standards may not be as high as Mrs Archer's, Roland determined, but he hoped at some point he could get them to be... more at ease in his service. It made him uncomfortable to think about how much control he had over the comfort and wellbeing of these people entrusted to his care, and he could not abide by the idea of abusing them—even in something as small as making them wait to eat until he decided to rise.

Thorne, of course, knew exactly how Roland's thoughts ran on this score. As Roland donned simple trousers and a shirt, Thorne helped him into the loose banyan that flowed over top.

"I also have some information regarding last night," he added as an extra impetus to head downstairs. "We can discuss it over breakfast."

The two made their way down the stairs to the formal dining table. It had been one of the first signs to Roland about how marriage would completely turn his life upside down. For the entirety of his time in London, Roland had eschewed the use of his father's dining room. When it was just the two of them in the house, they had shared a few meals in the kitchen.

But with Mrs Archer serving as cook, he had fewer reasons to eat out, and Albert and his wife would not be comfortable with him taking his meals in the kitchen—at least, not yet. It had taken some arguing, but Roland had found a compromise, even though it was still highly unconventional. He would consent to eat in the dining room only if Thorne would eat with him.

If they had thoughts about their new master's eccentricities, the butler and his wife kept them mostly to themselves. Likely, they assumed there was no reason to fuss over this temporary arrangement, because when Lady Charity joined his household, Thorne would no longer need to provide him with company at the table.

Roland's stomach soured again, and he sat down in the chair with something less than his usual grace.

Albert immediately brought a jug of small beer to them, and Thorne poured him a generous tot. "A hair of the dog what bit you."

"Thank you," he said to Thorne, and Thorne gripped his arm briefly in reply. The two said nothing more until Albert returned again, this time bearing plates of lightly buttered toast and cups holding soft boiled eggs.

Albert's hair ran pure white despite only being in his fifties, but the man looked steady, impeccable and serene. Roland studied him discreetly as he set down their food. "Thank you, Albert," he acknowledged politely when the man finished. Albert gave a small nod and departed, leaving them to their meal.

Examining his plate, Roland sighed briefly. "Did the whole house already know I was over-set?" he asked Thorne.

"It was an easy enough deduction to make when you were nearly sick on the stairs last night," Thorne's grin was wide enough to show most of his teeth.

Roland pulled a face. "I did not drink that much. But whisky and I do not seem to get along."

"I believe you. Be easy. You also had other things to turn your stomach."

He took another breath as he cracked his egg and stared into the yellow of the yolk. "Yes." Pushing the egg to the side, Roland instead helped himself to a piece of the toast.

Thorne got to business. "The servants at St James's have all been exonerated by dint of a thorough search, questioning, and by their continued presence. One could assume that a guilty party would make haste to leave before he could be discovered and sent to hang. I understand the questioning was not especially gentle." Roland nodded acknowledgment of this information. "As you suspected, few of the guests last night were willing to risk upset by leaving the table early. So it was a rather short list of guests who the servants took note of leaving the room before the reception began. Most guests waited until the break between to use the privacy rooms."

"Who is on the list?" he asked, though he already could name a few.

"You and Lady Grace, of course, were the first mentioned." Roland's lips flattened into a line. "The others on that list were Sir David Green, the dowager Lady Fitzroy, Lord Sebastian Vaughan, and Sir Julian Montgomery.

"And I suppose that list is in no particular order?" Roland asked.

"There was some disagreement about the order of departure," Thorne agreed. "All agree that Vaughan left first; Sir Julian, Sir David, and Lady Fitzroy left within close proximity to one another."

"I do not suppose their movements outside of the dinner room were tracked much?" Roland asked.

"Ah," said Thorne. "Well, only to an extent. All were seen entering the retiring rooms at some point during the dinner portion—except for you. Lady Grace, Lady Fitzroy and Sir Julian were also spotted by footmen taking short walks in other halls."

Roland remembered how Grace had reacted to finding the body. The feel of her pressed against his chest when he had spun her away, and the tremble of her body beneath his hands. "I think we can safely deduce that Grace was not the murderer.

*The Ruby Dagger*

And despite the fact that we despise the lady, I find it hard to imagine it was Lady Fitzroy."

"The woman was willing to poison Lady Charity," Thorne shrugged, raising his eyebrows. "I grant that poison is a better woman's weapon, but she would not be able to convince the guard to eat or drink something."

Roland scrubbed his cheek in disagreement. "You sound like Lady Grace. Even if Lady Fitzroy was willing to bloody her hands in this fashion, I find it difficult to believe she would have the strength to overpower an experienced guard and drive the dagger home. It was planted to the hilt, and cleanly too."

"Guile may make up for a lack of strength," the blue-eyed man shrugged.

Roland reluctantly conceded the point. "I suppose. Brute strength would not be the only way to move the guard from the hallway to inside the room. Mayhap he was convinced to move, or was investigating something. But then we have not narrowed the pool of suspects at all."

"Perhaps examining motivations will bring a suspect better to the fore. What reason would someone have for stealing such an identifiable item? It would not be money, surely, because attempting to fence such goods would out them immediately."

"One might pull the gems out of the dagger and sell them separately," Roland said, tracing a finger along the edge of his plate in thought. "But I concur, a need for money does seem to be an unlikely motive to steal that particular item."

Thorne had virtually inhaled his breakfast while Roland picked at his. Amused, Roland pushed the cooling egg his way, and Thorne began to eat that, too. At least then he wouldn't have Mrs Archer fussing.

"A political gift has political implications," Roland continued, musing to himself. "Could it be that someone wants to stir bad blood with Sweden?"

"If so, I do not know who has such hate for the Swedes," Thorne scratched the back of his head in thought. "We would have to learn more. Mayhap it is less that and more of an interest in embarrassing the crown?"

"In that case, Lady Fitzroy would be very much a suspect. But again, it seems dubious that she would do something that would so blatantly point in her direction. The others? I do not know their feelings about the crown."

"I will check on some of the jewellers just to be sure they did not receive rubies to fence. At any rate," Thorne added, "you have other things to do today, and you need to get dressed if you want to call upon Lady Charity in good time."

"Right. I had nearly forgotten." Roland sighed again, the toast sitting heavily in his stomach. He had to continue to woo his bride to be, and those matters needed to proceed apace.

# 7

Grace shifted her weight from one foot to the other, with a nervous smile flickering across her face as she listened for any sound from inside. Her hands fidgeted with the edges of her skirt, betraying her anxious anticipation. Her mama had a full day of calls planned, and had only agreed to this stop at Charity's home after extensive pleading from Grace.

The Cresswell's butler opened the door. His severe expression softened at the sight of Grace. "Good morning, Lady Grace. What a delight it is to have you reward us with your presence once again. Please, allow me to take your wrap and escort you to the garden, where Lady Charity awaits. I trust your journey here was as pleasant as the day is bright?"

"It is not a far distance to cover, as you well know, Bennett, but I appreciate your sentiments, nonetheless." Grace's nervous smile smoothed into one of true warmth as she handed her wrap to the butler and then followed him through the house. She had no need for his guidance, given her previous stay. Now that she was no longer a live-in guest, it would be inappropriate for her to wander the halls on her own.

She paid no mind to the framed portraits and paintings lining the walls, having long since studied them. They were perfectly in line with what one would expect, generations of Cresswell earls and ladies, their dour countenances captured for perpetuity. The landscapes in between showcased the highlights of the Cresswell estate in Surrey. Grace itched to sneak a Renaissance painting of cherubs visiting a round-bottomed woman into the mix, to see how long it would take anyone to notice. Such notions, however, would have to wait until Grace had a home of her own to decorate as she saw fit.

That prospect seemed years into the future, given her current status as an unattached debutante with no suitors. For Charity, however, if all went to plan, she would be living in the Northumberland townhouse before year end.

That thought soured Grace's mood. She banished it before it could do more damage. There were more important matters to address than why the thought of Charity's forthcoming marriage made her throat grow tight.

Charity sat in the bower in her garden, surrounded by roses in full bloom. The yellow and pink blossoms emphasised the golden strands in her hair and creamy, English rose skin. She glanced up from the book she was reading and grinned at the sight of Grace trailing behind the butler.

"Lady Grace for you, miss. Shall I have a footman bring around refreshments?" he asked before taking his leave.

"Some lemonade would be nice," Charity replied. "We will remain here to bask in the warmth and fresh air." She addressed her next words to Grace. "Come, sit beside me. I have hardly slept a wink due to all the questions swirling in my mind. You left me with the most tantalising hint and then rushed off."

"I did not dare to speak frankly in the palace," Grace countered, with a good-natured tone. She settled onto the

*The Ruby Dagger*

wrought-iron bench and tilted her head back to let the sun kiss her face.

Charity nudged her with her elbow. "You will get more freckles if you are not careful."

"I know. That is exactly what I am attempting to do. Perhaps with enough freckles, suitors will keep their attention elsewhere and I will not have to dance for the rest of the season." But Grace did as Charity instructed. She leaned over to glance at Charity's book and saw it was one of the romances her friend favoured. She did not pull a face, but it was a close one. "Now, where to begin? I must be succinct as I have little time to spend here, I am afraid. I must also find a way to get a message to Lord Percy so that we might agree on the first steps of our investigation."

"You have only to stay put to speak with the man yourself. He is due here within the hour for a short visit. I would be happy to play host to your conversation, if that is acceptable," Charity added. She did not notice the flash of pain that crossed Grace's face. "In truth, I wish he would stay longer. We are to be married, but I know so little of him. Perhaps he is simply a man of few words. Yet, if I am to be his wife, surely he must find some way to carry on a chat."

Grace had never thought Roland reticent to discuss anything, so she did not know what to say to Charity's complaint. If anything, it took her aback. Roland had opinions galore, as she had seen the night he came to dinner at her home, and in his interactions with the queen. But... He *did* hold some opinions about high society that would certainly be in contrast to Charity's view. Perhaps that was something of the problem after all—that he was afraid he would upset Charity, or simply did not know what else to say.

She left Charity's comments unanswered.

The footman arrived then, bearing the tray of refreshments.

He laid it upon a small, glass-topped table and then departed as silently as he had arrived. Grace leapt to her feet and poured them both a glass, her heightened energy needing some outlet. She passed one glass to Charity and held tight to her own as she paced the length of the bower.

"What I could not mention last night was that the ambassador's gift was stolen right from the throne room. I still can hardly believe it happened, Charity. The guard... we found him crumpled on his side, with a hunting knife still sticking from his chest."

"Stop there, I beg of you! I shall have nightmares if you go into more detail."

Grace arched an eyebrow at this remark, for Charity did not have a delicate constitution, nor was she prone to the vapours at the least hint of trouble.

"How did you come across the scene exactly?" Charity asked. "You and Lord Percy."

There was nothing to be gained by explaining they had entered the throne room simply because Grace feared being seen with him. "I told you, I stepped out for air and bumped into Lady Fitzroy when I returned. She... that viper of a woman gave me a tongue lashing, taunting me. Both you and me, truthfully," Grace said, afraid to look at Charity.

Charity, however, did not appear overwrought—much less surprised. "You were upset."

Grace nodded. "I lingered in the hallway, to gather myself. Lord Percy came upon me shortly thereafter. We were not far outside the throne room, so..." she trailed off to avoid lying directly to her. "We barely made it inside before we saw the guard... lying there. I admit I was not unmoved, but I soon pulled myself together. The rest, you mostly know. Lord Percy sent for the queen, and after some discussion, she agreed we should look into the matter. She is most determined to see the dagger returned without the ambassador learning of its absence."

"Yes, there is the risk he would take offence if discovered," Charity agreed.

The echo of footsteps interrupted them there. Bennett stepped from between a break in the hedge, with Roland following close behind. Was it Grace's imagination, or did he falter a step at the sight of her? If so, what did that mean?

By the time Bennett finished with the announcements and left, Roland was once again imperturbable, with a pleasant, if vacant, expression upon his face. He bowed first to Charity and then to Grace. "Good morning, my ladies. I hope I am not interrupting your visit."

"Not at all. We were expecting you," Charity replied. She shifted ever so slightly, emphasising the space beside her on the bench. Roland shifted uncomfortably from side to side, his gaze skipping between Grace and Charity.

This was not a difficult choice. The man was engaged to Charity, and should be hurrying to take the space at her side. Indeed, given the little amount of time they had away from the prying eyes of the ton, he should be taking her hand in his and staring into her eyes.

Charity's brow creased as his awkward stance remained longer than it should. Grace could not bear to see her friend unhappy, so she took it upon herself to point Roland in the right direction.

"Please, do take a seat, Lord Percy. I think better on my feet, but there is no need for you to stand on ceremony."

Roland looked as though he had been caught out, and he hurried over to sit on the bench. But Grace noted he took great care to leave a clear gap between himself and his intended bride.

Sitting with the two women, Roland gripped his leg to avoid the urge to run his hand nervously through his hair, trying to think of how to make the situation less awkward. "Your, er, gardens here are lovely, Lady Charity. Do you do much gardening yourself?"

"I do not, Lord Percy. All the accolades must be given to our gardener," she replied with a small smile that did not reach her eyes. As the pause between them lengthened, she ventured, "Do you have gardens at your property?"

"Not... not really," he admitted. Like many townhouses in London, his had a small private space at the back, but it had patently suffered from years of neglect and Mrs Archer did not have any time for it. He did not want to admit the shortcomings of his household to her, but on the other hand, even 'Sir Barbarian' knew that such a brief answer was rude. He made a short attempt at humor. "The house was my father's before it became mine. It seems he was not much of a gardener either."

"Then maybe we can borrow Mr. Thompson after we get married," she said, her smile warming a little. "A small townhouse should not be any trouble for him to look after, in addition to serving my parents."

"I—" Roland's gaze snagged upon Grace, who was giving him a look of disbelief. He closed his eyes then. He had to do better than this. "Yes, Lady Charity, that would be a wonderful idea. I have been slow in finding more hired hands for my place. There has been so much happening that I have not had time to tend to it."

Lady Charity was too canny to miss the glance her friend had given Roland at his stilted conversation, and abruptly, she brought the matter to a head. "Faith, this is awkward with the two of you dancing around what happened. Lord Percy, I know the queen has set the two of you to investigate the possibility that someone in the ton is responsible for the theft and murder.

*The Ruby Dagger*

I understand you likely need to share information with each other."

Grace looked mildly conflicted. "But Charity, you are supposed to be courting—"

"Please. I would rather aid you. If all I can do to help is give you a safe place to talk and maintain decency, then I will assist however I can."

Roland relaxed, glad that no one had to continue talking about gardens, weddings, or sewing. "Lady Grace, the servants and other guardsmen were cleared of suspicion, leaving only the list of people who left the dinner. It is a short one. Sir Julian Montgomery, Sir David Green, Lord Sebastian Vaughan, and Lady Fitzroy."

At that, Grace lost her reluctant expression. "We already know *she* left. I saw her in the hallway. I still think she had somewhat to do with it."

"I do not think so, Lady Grace. Thorne says that a footman near the refreshment rooms vouched for her being rather expedient in her absence. She was memorable; apparently she dropped her fan, and she asked him to retrieve it for her."

"But he may have lied for her," Grace argued. "In such case, she would have had time to attack the guard."

Roland fidgeted, since talking about bodies was most certainly unsuitable for ladies and surely would earn him a lecture from Thorne. Possibly Albert, too. He suspected the two of them bonded over fussing over his manners like nursemaids. "At the expense of being ungentlemanly... the manner of the guard's death... Gr—Lady Grace, I do not think so. Not only would it likely require a feat of strength a woman does not possess, the dowager is too clever to do something so ham-fisted."

Grace's eyes flared, but Charity, who was looking thoughtful, stayed her retort with a finger. "I agree with Lord

Percy, Grace. There does not seem to be a clear benefit in her committing murder to steal the ambassador's gift."

"Unless she wanted to send a message." Huffing, Grace subsided. "Fine, I take your point. We should not fail to consider the other suspects. But I do not know any of these men except by name. Do you?"

"I've been acquainted with Sir David Green for years," Roland murmured. "He was my first superior officer, but he also recently retired from the position of Commander-in-Chief. The queen sent him to assist me after you departed."

"That makes sense," Lady Charity nodded, but when Grace looked confused, she expanded. "If he had experience serving in the palace, he would be familiar with its defences and the guards."

"And could be trusted to be discreet," Roland added.

"What did he learn?" Grace asked him.

"He was the one conducting the interrogations of the staff, and he was the one to contact the coroner. He was going to check the hunting knife for a maker's mark once the coroner removed it from the body, but on that, I have not heard anything."

Seeing Charity's pale face, he deftly switched back to the list of gentlemen. "I also am not acquainted with Sir Julian Montgomery," Roland admitted. "Or Lord Sebastian Vaughan, for that matter. Thorne is collecting more information for me this afternoon."

"Lord Vaughan is one of the more prominent members of the Society of Antiquaries," Lady Charity said, a delicate frown forming between her brows. "My father has done dealings with him. He is a collector of ancient jewellery and regalia. Sir Julian Montgomery..." she shook her head. "His reputation is that he is a very stuffy man. Hopefully, your Thorne can provide more information about him."

*The Ruby Dagger*

"A gift from a king could be something Lord Vaughan would be interested in, if he has a private collection," Grace said reluctantly. "Perhaps we will see these men at upcoming events, and we could question them discreetly."

"Perhaps you can," Lady Charity said wryly. "My invitations these last two weeks have been rather limited."

"In spite of the queen's proclamations about your virtue?" Grace said, aghast. Roland also frowned. He had seen a few sideways looks at dinner, but he had not realised that Lady Charity's reputation was still so fragile.

"Stop. The both of you," Lady Charity said, shifting her gaze between them. "This will pass with time. Lord Percy's courtship of me has already been immensely helpful in putting wagging tongues to rest. Time and marriage will silence the rest, as long as we do not stir any further trouble."

She exchanged a meaningful glance with her friend. "The risk of my disgrace means I may not be able to help you."

"You need not—"

She smiled at Grace fully, knowing how much her next words would pain her friend. "You must come to the forefront, Grace. It falls upon you to navigate the social waters with charm and aplomb in my place as you unravel this mystery." And raising an eyebrow at her awkward suitor, she added, "Both of you."

# 8

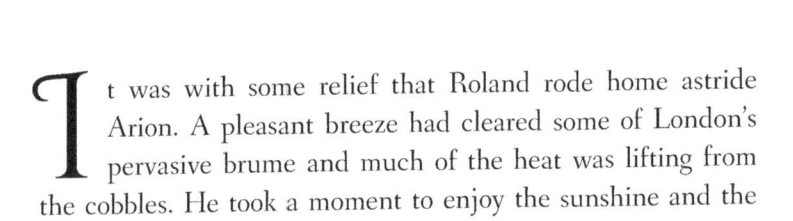

It was with some relief that Roland rode home astride Arion. A pleasant breeze had cleared some of London's pervasive brume and much of the heat was lifting from the cobbles. He took a moment to enjoy the sunshine and the relative freedom found in Arion's clattering trot.

Wes greeted him and took the reins when he returned home. It had been a strange adjustment, getting accustomed to the new faces in the house, but if pressed, he would admit he was coming to enjoy it. Like the warp and weft of a loom, his house was coming together in an orderly pattern. It was gradually feeling more like a home—a sensation he couldn't remember having for a long, long time.

He gave the lad a pat upon his head, noting he did indeed seem much cleaner now under Albert's wife's supervision. Perhaps Mrs Archer was right in her assertions after all, that men—and boys too—were unable to clean anything.

She was making headway, clearly. But the boy still was a little grubby behind his ears.

Albert greeted him at the doorstep and took his greatcoat.

*The Ruby Dagger*

"Thorne is waiting for you in the study," he told Roland. "Shall I bring you tea?"

Roland's steps hesitated. "Thank you, Albert. For now, no tea. I will stop by the kitchen later, perhaps."

Albert's thick, bushy eyebrows crawled up his forehead. "My lord..."

"I know. I am an uncivilised, simple man who has done much for himself and is still not accustomed to being waited on. Be patient with me, Albert. Your service is not at fault in the smallest degree."

His butler's wounded indignation clearly deflated a little. "Sir Harold was much the same as you in some regards. Early on. I insist you ring for me if you change your mind."

"Certainly," he assured the older man, and made his way inside. Hopeful that Thorne had found some helpful information, he hurried to join him. Thorne was seated at Roland's desk, writing out a message.

"Thorne," Roland breathed. "Any luck?"

Getting up with alacrity, Thorne's brow creased. "I am sorry. I should not have taken liberties using your desk, but the other desks have no supplies and I have not—I have not purchased my own yet."

Roland blinked at him, taken aback. Why were the members of his household getting so prickly about propriety as of late? "You require no explicit permission to use mine. Surely you know I would not care if you use my desk for writing correspondence."

"No—But I should. You will marry soon, and I should be careful about being too familiar. Lady Charity would not be happy about it."

The thought that Lady Charity could take it upon herself to discipline Thorne for any reason filled him with coldness. He would have to make certain she was aware Thorne enjoyed any unusual liberties with Roland's full approval. Happily, he would extend some of these to the others as well. So far, they had refused additional privileges beyond the purchase of some clothing, but they had not spent ten years working closely with Roland as Thorne had.

"Cease with this nonsense," Roland scolded him. "I find it difficult to believe she could be so hard-hearted. I will make sure she understands you may use my desk to write to your mother whenever you wish."

"Or we could purchase some more inkwells and quills," Thorne joked, but it fell flat.

Roland frowned at Thorne, noticing that he was unusually tense. "Is all well at home?"

The man looked down at the floor, deliberating, and then he met Roland's gaze and shrugged. "As well as can be expected. A cough that is lingering, but it is getting better as the summer waxes. But never mind that. I looked into your list of men."

Reluctantly, he let the subject drop. His grandfather had ceased all threats of financial penalties since the banns had been posted. That alone was the only reason that he felt comfortable hiring a butler and housekeeper. Nevertheless, concerns about finances were familiar to him. He had long suspected that Thorne had been sending his wages on. "I spoke with Lady Charity about the list too. She said that Sebastian Vaughan was a collector of some sort. Jewellery and such?"

"Aye, a rather notorious one at that." At Roland's look of surprise, Thorne regained some of his usual humour. "Though to be fair, the man doesn't collect only jewellery. He has a number of collections of various obscure, priceless, and unique artefacts. The more difficult to obtain, the more valuable he considers it."

"I see," Roland said. "So one could argue he might be

*The Ruby Dagger*

motivated to acquire a ceremonial dagger, even going to such great lengths?"

"It would be a gamble for him, but yes. One of his prize artefacts is a circlet that belonged to some 10th-century Byzantine Empress. Or so he has claimed."

Musing over this, Roland drummed his fingers on the door frame. "Most men like to display their wealth. Has much of his collection been seen?"

"As I understand it, that is one of the bones of contention in his society. Lord Vaughan is like many gentlemen, fond of displaying his wealth when it comes to funding his expeditions. But as for his collection, rumour has it that he is more like a dragon sitting upon his treasures. There have been squabbles between him and some of the members of the society about the results of some of his shared ventures. I doubt Lady Charity would have heard that part."

"Hmm," Roland said. "Though Lady Charity has heard of him. He must show some hint of generosity if the women of society know him."

"Yes. As I understand, he is popular with the ladies involved in philanthropy. Often he is willing to donate an old artefact that no longer pleases him when he has found a new precious item to coo over. In fact, word is he will be donating one to a bazaar tomorrow."

"What of Sir David Green? What was he about? Maybe he saw something that can help."

Thorne scratched his eyebrow, frowning. "Unlike the others, Sir David was called away from the table. And not just once, but twice. Once by a footman from the hallway, and the other by the queen."

Roland wondered what a footman had wanted of the man. "I assume that the queen's request came when she sent him to meet with me."

"I believe so, as this was shortly before people were invited to head to the reception."

"I do not suppose you know anything about the former? Why would a footman come for him?"

Thorne grimaced. "I do not know, but there is every possibility that it was an official matter. He spoke with the security staff several times that night."

"Agreed." Roland leaned against the door frame. "Were you able to find out more about Lady Fitzroy? Or what of Sir Julian Montgomery?"

"Nothing more on Lady Fitzroy than I've already learned. Sir Julian Montgomery... well." Thorne looked uncertain. "He went to the refreshment room also, but unlike the others who did, he was notable by the fact that he was gone the longest. He also bade the servant stationed inside to leave him be for the duration."

That was curious, but not unusually so, to wish for privacy. "How long was he away from the table?"

"As best I can determine, about half of an hour. And Roland... his chosen room had another exit."

Roland thought about that for a bit. Sir Julian Montgomery would have been spotted leaving by the usual route... but St James's Palace was riddled with back corridors and stairwells. It wasn't improbable that a thief with an agenda might make use of them. It was not by any means a concrete piece of evidence, but it was a possibility that had to be considered. Especially given that his time away would have afforded someone the most advantage in committing a murder and taking the dagger.

"Is that all?" he finally asked Thorne. "Stop shuffling about and speak up if there is something more to tell about him."

Thorne ceased shifting from foot to foot. "Just a spot of rumour. I don't know how credible it is. The servants, by the

*The Ruby Dagger*

way, are gossiping and speculating heavily on the identity of the murderer. They favour Sir Julian Montgomery as the culprit."

"Because of the amount of time he spent in the retiring room?" Roland raised an eyebrow. Surely there had to be more to it than that.

"That, and also it is said that there is bad blood between Sir Julian Montgomery and the ambassador. I have been given to understand they were seen exchanging words on more than one occasion."

Roland wasn't certain what connections could lie between the Swedish Baron Gustaf Albin Lindberg and a titled English nobleman. They weren't of a similar enough age to have attended a college together, and the baron was reputed to be a diplomat his whole life long, whereas Montgomery, as far as Roland was aware, was also career military. "Bad enough blood that it could be a possible motive for theft?"

Thorne hitched one shoulder in a shrug.

"So," Roland sighed, finally settling on the couch. "A loose gaggle of possible motivations—some scarcely more than opportunities. Nothing that rules any of them out for certain."

"At least the suspect pool is somewhat limited," Thorne pointed out. "The servants have been cleared of suspicion. It might have been much worse."

The effort Roland and Grace made for Lady Charity had felt more like searching for a needle in a haystack, and Roland had no wish to repeat that experience. "I do hope then that the true culprit is entangled in this net."

"Aye," Thorne agreed in such a heartfelt tone that Roland's mood lightened a bit. Thorne's thoughts appeared to be in exactly the same place.

Pulling his attention back to the matter at hand, Roland wondered what to do next. "So now comes the task of questioning them discreetly, hopefully without causing much offence. I believe you said that Vaughan was attending some charity bazaar tomorrow?"

His man brightened. "Yes. It was planned to coincide with a military parade tomorrow at the Horse Guards Parade. A demonstration of the might of the British empire to impress the baron, I believe. I was hoping you would want to go."

A good military parade would be a more enjoyable way to spend time in London than a ball, for certain. "You miss the service as much as I do, then?" Roland teased him.

"It certainly was a simpler way of life," Thorne confessed. "Although I will admit, the beds here are better."

Grinning, Roland agreed. "I think we should attend this parade. But what of Lord Vaughan? He is our best suspect."

"You might write ahead and leave him to Lady Grace," Thorne suggested. "You don't really wish to go to a ladies' bazaar, do you? Besides, the ambassador will be in attendance as the guest of honour. It may be a good chance to investigate the cause of Montgomery's ruffled feathers."

"A fair point. And if we are fortunate, perhaps one of the others will be available for discreet inquiry."

# 9

The next day, Grace made a last check of her hair in the mirror of her dressing table. Elsie stood behind her, holding a hand mirror so that Grace could see the twists she had plaited into her hair. The style was more elaborate than the ones Grace usually favoured, but Grace did not complain. Elsie was determined to prove her worth as a proper lady's maid and had been practising styles under the tutelage of the head maid.

"Will it do, miss?" Elsie asked when her patience ran out. "You will be out most of the day, moving around the event. I did not want to chance your hair tumbling down at an inopportune moment."

"If you think my hair is any more obedient than the rest of me, you need less time with the curling tongs and more time at my side. But that aside, yes, it looks lovely." Grace resisted the urge to touch her hair. She raised her gaze until she met Elsie's eyes in the mirror. "While I am out for the day, might you be willing to run an errand for me?"

"Of course, my lady. Did you need something from the modiste? Or more paper and ink?"

"I have something different in mind," Grace said. She pushed her stool back and shifted around until she was facing Elsie. She pointed Elsie toward the nearby chair and waited until the maid sat down. "Between the late night at the palace and the busy day, I have not had time to tell you what has happened."

Elsie's eyes widened, and she momentarily lost her composure, clutching at the seat of her wooden chair as Grace recounted the murder and her subsequent rise into the role of investigator. "Again, miss? And Lord Percy was there with you?"

"He happened upon me," Grace corrected her maid. "Now we are to work together again. If you can get away, please go to visit Thorne so that you two can arrange the means for exchanging regular messages."

Elsie's countenance brightened. "I wouldn't mind checking on the children—the Sprouts, as Thorne calls them. I'm sure he's taking good care of them, but I'll feel better for checking it with my own eyes."

"Thank you. I was fortunate to cross paths with Roland while at Charity's yesterday, but I cannot depend on fortune's whims moving forward."

Elsie bit her lip and fiddled with the edge of her apron. Grace waved a hand for her to get on with it. "What does Lady Charity think of you spending time with his lordship?"

"We are hardly meeting one another for pleasure, Elsie. He and I are invested in finding the truth, albeit for our own reasons. There is no sentiment involved."

"Then why are you doing this, miss? It is hardly seemly for a debutante to involve herself in such matters."

"And I am hardly the picture of the average debutante. I need more in my life. Roland understands that, as does the queen. That is why she is allowing me to take part in the matter."

"If you ask me, it is passing strange that his lordship is so willing to encourage you... and that Lady Charity doesn't mind you speaking so often with her betrothed. Your ways seem so foreign at times like this."

Grace did not take offence at her maid's words. Sometimes the gulf between their stations widened past the point of comprehension. That was all that was happening now. She and Roland were clear on where they stood with one another. He was to marry Charity. Nothing else mattered.

Elsie stood and busied herself gathering Grace's wrap, gloves, and hat. Within short order, Grace climbed into the family carriage to sit across from her mama. Their driver, Grantham, twitched the reins to encourage the horses to set off at a steady pace. The carriage wheels bumped over the rough cobblestone, but the women felt little discomfort thanks to the padded upholstered seats inside.

"We are fortunate Lady Melbourne agreed to host at Melbourne House today, for I fear the weather will not hold much past afternoon. To think, Mrs Dixon suggested we set up stalls along the edge of St James's Park." Lady Tilbury sniffed in disapproval. "Money she may have, but she lacks the breeding to understand the refined requirements of the ton."

Grace turned to face the window so her mother would not catch her rolling her eyes. Breeding was no guarantee of good choices. Lady Fitzroy had an impeccable lineage, but that had not stopped her from kidnapping Charity. And maybe now doing worse. Although, that remained to be proven.

Grantham joined the line of carriages waiting to disgorge their passengers near Whitehall. Between the horse guard parade and the charity bazaar, the wide street was teeming with carriages and phaetons. Even the lone men on horseback struggled to pass by. Grace wrinkled her nose as the heavy summer air carried in the stench of the Thames and the earthy smell of manure.

Her mother pulled a scented handkerchief from her cuff and passed it to Grace. "You must have a word with Elsie. She should have provided you with a scented cloth for just such moments. She has come a fair way, but there is still room for improvement."

In this, Grace was in agreement. The sharp scent of lavender cleared her head. She did not relinquish it until it was their turn to descend. The butler welcomed the women into Melbourne House and, after taking their wraps, showed them through to the rear of the mansion where the event was to be held.

For an event designed to collect funds for military widows and their children, a significant amount had been spent on creating a lavish setting appropriate for the upper class attendees. Silk-covered boxes sat on wooden pedestals on either side of each entrance, waiting to collect the entrance donations. After Lady Tilbury deposited the expected amount into the nearest one, the women entered the fray.

Society women wearing muslin day dresses and elegantly tailored spencers mingled in small groups throughout the space. Tables lined the walls and marched across the middle of the room, displaying various items for purchase or bidding. One held hand-painted ceramic platters from Italy, another hand-tatted lace. A string quartet played in the next room over, providing a soothing tone to block the neighing of horses outside.

Grace allowed her mother to take the lead until they had paid their regards to their host and the leaders of the benevolent society. That task accomplished, Lady Tilbury granted Grace permission to wander on her own, providing she observed all the rules of society.

"I shall endeavour not to allow myself to be trapped in the embrace of a rake, Mama, no matter how handsome he may be," Grace promised, fluttering her lashes. Her mother bit back a heated retort and allowed a harsh glare to communicate her displeasure with Grace's sass.

Grace adopted an angelic pose and walked off before her mother could retract her permission. The first table that caught her eye was one bearing tiny glass bottles of scent. Grace ambled over, taking no note of who else was near. Such was that she found herself in close quarters with Lark Fitzroy.

"Good afternoon, Lady Grace. I have not had the chance to speak with you since you so kindly paid us a visit after our ball."

Grace stiffened at the young woman's words. She had paid that call on the Fitzroy family in the hopes of learning more about Charity's disappearance. At the time, she had no idea how close she was to the truth. Even now, she was unsure whether Lark was complicit in the kidnapping, or completely unaware. As such, she hesitated over long before offering a reply, and Lady Lark carried on.

"Of course, you were well occupied for a time, were you not? Lord Percy claimed much of your attention while Lady Charity was away. So much so that one wondered if he had turned his head in a new direction." She tilted her head prettily and looked through her lashes. "Yet, here you stand on your own."

"Indeed," Grace said, surprising herself with how perfectly pleasant she sounded. "Lord Percy was kind to me during my hour of need, and we both count ourselves fortunate that Lady Charity was safe and sound during her absence."

Lark wrinkled her nose but held her tongue. Grace half-wished she had said more, for she still had no idea of Lark's involvement. Had she known of the plot against Charity? Or was she simply following her mama's guidance to cast aspersions on Charity's return? There was only one way to find out.

With that in mind, she latched arms with Lark and guided her deeper into the room. "Come, Lady Lark, let us not speak of such difficult times. We are here, with so many items on display for our consideration. Let us have a walk about and catch up on our latest ongoings while we peruse."

Under ceilings painted with allegories of the virtues, Grace searched for any hint of vice and malice. She quizzed Lark about her recent engagements, opinions on various suitors, and invitations to upcoming balls. Very slowly, she worked her way around to her topic of primary interest.

"Tell me, Lady Lark, did you and your family enjoy dinner at the palace this week?"

Lark sniffed. "The meat course arrived cold."

"Really? Mine was piping hot. Perhaps it was because of how far down the table you sat from me," Grace replied, getting in a subtle dig over the Fitzroys come-down at court. "And the ceremonial dagger? Did you get a close look at it?"

"Only in passing. My mama has plenty of rubies in her jewellery collection, and I have no interest in weapons."

Grace grit her teeth at Lark's short remarks. She glanced around for inspiration, seeing only the refreshment tables heaped with cream buns and miniature sandwiches. She roamed wider until she spied Lady Fitzroy in discussion with a pair of men she did not recognise.

One man stood behind a table decorated with antiques, silver, and small paintings. His staid suit suggested he was a local dealer rather than a guest. Lady Fitzroy and the other man had their eyes fixed on a golden locket displayed on a black velvet cushion.

*The Ruby Dagger*

"I see your mama is here, but I do not recognise the man beside her. Is he a friend of your family?"

Lark shook her head. "Even my brother would not bother with such a known dandy as Lord Sebastian Vaughan. The man's interest only extends to items he can buy or win. His collection of curiosities has no rival. Not even the crown," she added.

Grace could hardly believe her luck, as this was exactly the man Roland had suggested she meet. That he stood with Lady Fitzroy made him all the more interesting as a potential suspect in the crime. But before she could suggest to Lark they stray closer, Lady Fitzroy raised her hands and backed away from the table, leaving the locket to Lord Vaughan.

"I should go to Mama," Lark said, slipping free. "She does so hate to lose out on things once she gets her mind set, and it would seem she was outbid for the locket. I shall have to distract her with something else."

Lark dashed off, leaving Grace standing on her own. People milled around her, but none stopped to talk, so caught up were they in viewing the items for sale. And so, Grace lingered where she was, across the room from Lord Vaughan, with a clear line of sight. She watched as the dealer procured a small box from beneath the table and wrapped the locket in cloth.

Lord Vaughan reached into his coat pocket, presumably to retrieve his pocketbook. But instead, he pulled free a wrapped packet of his own. He glanced left and right and then handed it to the dealer. Without a word, the man slipped the package under the table and then carried on with the sale of the locket.

What had that been about? Desperation to see under the table clawed at the back of Grace's throat, but she could find no way to do so. The white cloth hung to the floor, hiding everything behind and underneath the table. She briefly considered feigning a tumble and tugging on the cloth on her way up, but soon abandoned the notion. In retaliation for embarrassing the family, her mama might blockade her in the house, or worse yet, marry her off to the first man who walked past.

Lord Vaughan stalked off in the opposite direction and exited into the gardens. Grace picked up her pace and hurried to catch up. She arrived in time to see him exit the courtyard on the far side, heading off to the horse guard parade happening outside.

Still, the day was not a total wash. She would report back to Roland about what she had seen. Mayhap Thorne could pay the dealer a visit and find the information another way.

# 10

"Stop fussing with your collar, Sir Barbarian," Thorne growled at Roland in a low tone that wouldn't be overheard in the crowd. "You will muss your cravat. And then what would all these lords and ladies think of the sheer indignity of that?"

Roland dropped his hands, restraining the urge to scowl. "I am half strangled in it, *Mama*." But he left the cravat alone and occupied his hands with straightening his dark blue riding coat. It was quite fine, cut of a light wool, with some subtle silver braiding along the cuffs and edges as a nod to his service.

Perhaps uncharacteristically for London, the weather was holding fine and a touch warm to boot. The pea gravel of the parade grounds and the white stone of the nearby buildings of the mall reflected the sun and heat back into the waiting crowds. Standing where they were, the two men were too far away to enjoy the verdant green and relative cool breeze of St James's Park. A light sheen of sweat dotted the brows of many of the gentlemen nearby, but it didn't dampen their anticipation.

The royalty and some select guests, including the

ambassador, had been invited to mingle close to Whitehall. Roland had found himself in possession of an invitation, and he planned to make his way there afterwards. For now, he wished to be nothing more than a simple man reminiscing on his service, enjoying the parade and the company of the man whom he had trusted to guard his back for more than ten years.

That was his plan, at any rate. As they waited, his thoughts wandered. He and Thorne had passed by the home where the women were setting up the bazaar earlier. Grace hadn't yet been there, and he wondered if she would have any luck with shreds of gossip among the ladies, or manage to converse somehow with Sebastian Vaughan.

But the rhythmic clatter of hooves pulled his thoughts away as the rows of cavalrymen made their entrance. All heads nearby turned to appreciate the horses, immaculately groomed, their coats gleaming, as they trotted by in neat rows.

Ah, he missed this! The glory, and the purpose in it. Thorne, too, appeared to be observing with a hint of longing. Was this envy he felt as he watched the riders sitting tall in the saddle, their silver sabres and regimental colours glinting? It already almost seemed like a different life, and his chest grew hollow as he wondered whether he would be able to return. Someday.

The crowd thinned as the people dispersed to gain a better view of the manoeuvres. Thorne jostled him out of his melancholy thoughts and pointed with his chin. Over the heads of the people, he could see the royal family on a raised stand. Squinting at it, he could make out the queen and what must have been the figures of the Prince Regent and the ambassador. Beside the stand surely must be Prince Frederick, Duke of York, to judge by the feathered bicorn. He was seated upon his own massive midnight black stallion which had been curried so that it fairly gleamed in the sunlight. The powerful beast must have

*The Ruby Dagger*

been at least sixteen hands tall and was clearly unhappy to not be joining his fellows, to judge by the eager prancing as they watched the tactical displays.

Nodding at Thorne, he began to cautiously wind his way through the crowd in that direction, closer to Whitehall. The guards standing by took note of his approach, and once they had ascertained his invitation to be there, had him escorted to join the rest of the nobility ensconced therein.

"Roland," a voice greeted him, and he turned to find a familiar face indeed, also dressed in his full uniform.

"Sir David," Roland replied, giving his commander a bow. "It is good to see you again. Are you here as a guest of the Queen?"

"The Prince Regent, actually," Sir David Green nodded with a wry grin. "As I had been of such great assistance the other evening, I have been given the august task of acting as advisor for certain... diplomatic functions. I believe it was His Royal Highness the Prince Regent's way of making sure I could be at hand—should other unfortunate events happen, or should members of the gentry decide to behave inappropriately."

Roland couldn't help but smile in return at the man's tone. "A job well done has its own rewards."

"A phrase more true has never been spoken. Are you enjoying the parade?"

"Yes, and I think Thorne is, too. I left him on the farther edges of the grounds," Roland said. "He remembers you fondly."

"I know," Green said with a smile. "I spoke with him briefly that evening, when we were discussing the servants. He has grown to be as strapping as you, and then some. It is too bad, that matter—" Halting that train of thought at Roland's sudden tension, the man changed the subject, making a face of distaste. "Well, I suppose the past is the past, and we should concern ourselves more with matters of the now, like standing on ceremony and ensuring we maintain our good graces with the royal family."

Roland wondered what Sir David Green had been about to say. "It sounds as though you are regretting setting foot back in London."

"In spades," Green said dryly. "To think I had originally come here to deal with my solicitor and take care of a few financial interests! Ah, well. Retirement had been somewhat dull, I admit. So perhaps this should be more of a cautionary tale: be careful in wishing for more excitement in your life. I trust you are also following your own line of investigations? The servants' trail is cold; any who left were all kept busy pouring wine all night for the head table or went directly back to their post. And the weapon was also fruitless. I suppose the murderer leaving some sign leading directly back to him would have made things too easy."

"I did have hopes of speaking to some of the other missing members of the dinner party, were they here." Green nodded his understanding. "Perhaps I could also find a moment to speak with the ambassador and peruse his thoughts on the matter."

Green lifted his hand in negation. "You cannot. At least, you cannot yet. The Prince Regent has not yet told him."

"He still has not told him? Why ever not?" Roland asked.

Shifting uneasily, Green cast his eyes about, no doubt ensuring that they had enough privacy to not be overheard. "You know the queen and Prince Regent were hoping we could find the stolen item again quickly enough that it need never be mentioned. Bide a while longer. That period of grace should expire shortly, and they will be forced to inform the ambassador —but they will do so in their own time."

He understood that the royal family would no doubt prefer to pretend nothing had ever happened. Still, it would impede

*The Ruby Dagger*

his ability to follow certain lines of questioning. "All right," he agreed more graciously than he felt. "If I find myself in conversation with the ambassador, I shall avoid making mention of it. Perhaps I should speak with the Prince Regent instead, if I have the chance."

Sir David spotted the Prince Regent on the far side of the cluster and inclined his head in that direction. Lowering his voice, he said, "Yonder. I see Prinny in the company of some of his rakehell friends. Good luck, my young friend," Sir David added. "I need to speak with a few others myself, so I must continue on my way. However, if I can ever be of aid, you have only to ask."

"Thank you, Sir David," Roland said, bidding his old colonel a farewell.

Looking back in the direction of Prinny, Roland could not discern who the Prince Regent was standing with, but perhaps he could angle that way and get a better view. As he stepped around small clusters of various dignitaries and military men he did not know, his path took him unexpectedly towards the ambassador and another man standing nearby.

Roland had only the briefest of meetings with Ambassador Baron Gustaf Albin Lindberg the evening of the presentation, but the man was just as imposing as he remembered. Perhaps it was somewhat in the way he spoke—his English was meticulous but as cold and precise as a blade, and it seemed that the man standing there was the target of its edge.

"—you dare to impose upon me with your presence."

"How could I not, Lindberg? This is my home. My country. I have no need to cower."

The two exuded an air of such tense hostility that Roland paused, watching them from the corner of his eye under the pretence of studying the horses. Both men stood casually, also looking off at the parade. But at the one man's words, Lindberg turned to face him more fully.

"Perhaps you should, Montgomery. Were I responsible for what you have done, I would certainly hesitate to give my patrons the opportunity to reveal my nature. Excuse me."

Lindberg was in such a fluster that he nearly brushed against Roland in his haste to depart, and Roland stepped politely aside to avoid the collision. The other man, he realised, looking at him in a new light, must be Sir Julian Montgomery. Roland recalled seeing the man at the dinner, but had not spoken with him. And it was clear that the two knew each other rather well. Lindberg clearly felt no need to address him with the honour the title should have deserved.

For that matter, Sir Julian had showed a similar level of disrespect—well unexpected for a gentleman. Thorne had said the two had exchanged words more than once; that appeared to be an understatement of their animosity.

Roland sized the man up. Sir Julian was in his late fifties, his hair more grey with age than not. Perhaps at one time he might have been fit, but if so, he had gone rather soft with age and a nobleman's lifestyle.

"I must admit, Earl Percy, it is a rather novel experience to receive such a reception to my arrival."

The droll words were uttered by a masculine voice. Startled, Roland glanced directly into the face of the Prince of Wales. "Forgive me, Your Highness. I was thinking of a strange encounter with the ambassador and did not hear you approach."

The Prince Regent straightened a little. "Strange how? Have you had any luck with your investigation?"

"In truth, not yet, sir. I only noticed that the ambassador appeared to be upset by Sir Julian Montgomery's presence, and they exchanged words of some heat. Do you know why they are at odds with one another?"

*The Ruby Dagger*

Prinny flapped his hand, not interested in the least. "There is some long-standing old feud between them from something that happened years past. I know not what; it is of no import."

Hesitating, Roland thought his words over carefully. "Do you believe it has no import to his motivations for leaving the table that evening at dinner?"

Prinny's eyes flared briefly at Roland's questioning, but he considered it with due thought. "It may explain some rudeness that evening," he allowed. "However, if you are seeking reasons for the ambassador's state of mind now, there is another reason he may be out of sorts."

"Is there? Did something happen earlier, sir?" Roland asked the Prince Regent.

"He is now aware that his diplomatic gift has... gone astray."

Roland took a breath in surprise. "Sir David Green warned me off questioning the ambassador earlier. He said the ambassador was not yet aware of the theft."

Prinny inclined his head slightly. "In the man's defence, Sir David quite certainly did not knowingly play you false. The ambassador was only just now informed—and unfortunately, the deed was done by way of the careless slip of someone else's tongue."

"I see," Roland murmured. Small wonder then, that the ambassador was wroth.

Prinny raked his eyes over Roland, and then continued. "We have informed him we are doing everything within our means to see it returned. You are doing your part to vouchsafe my words, Lord Percy?"

"It is slow going because the discussions must be delicate, Your Highness, but yes, I am making steady progress—" Roland's words faltered as his eyes went to seek Sir Julian's position, and he found the man gone. Inwardly, he cursed. "I am making progress in questioning the missing diners, sir."

"As you were, then," Prinny said, amused. Clearly, a dismissal.

Roland backed away from the Prince Regent with care, discreetly casting his gaze around the throng of select guests. But Sir Julian, apparently, had left. The day passed without any further illuminations.

# 11

The following morning, Grace woke far earlier than normal, her mind too busy considering suspects and motives to allow her to rest. The barest hint of the pale dawn light crept around the edge of the velvet drapes. In another hour, sunlight would tighten its hold and make any hope of further rest impossible. Not that it mattered.

The fireplace was bare; the day promising to be too warm to make a fire necessary. Grace grabbed her wrapper from where it lay at the foot of her bed and shrugged it on. She ventured over to her writing table, with the intention to pen a note for Elsie to carry on her behalf. Roland needed to be made aware of Lord Vaughan's curious behaviour at the bazaar. What had he passed over to the antique dealer? The package had seemed too small to hold the missing dagger. But what if he had already removed the gemstones? They alone would take up little space.

She got no further than reaching for her favourite swan quill before she drew up short.

She did not want to send Elsie in her place. She wanted to go in person, to discuss each possibility and what action they should take next. The image of the pair of them sitting in Roland's study took hold and refused to budge.

She glanced at the clock again and ran through the calculations. Her mother never rose before ten, believing anything earlier to be unladylike. It was why Grace was in the habit of remaining in her room until later in the morning. If she snuck out now, no one would notice. She would have to be fairly quick, two hours and no more than that. But it was feasible. If she hurried... and had some help.

She rang for Elsie. Her maid arrived in very short order, bearing a tray laden with hot chocolate and a stack of buttered bread. Grace bade her to sit and explained her plan.

"We are going to trade places. Wearing your uniform and cap, I am going to dash out for a brief errand. In my absence, I need you to stay here."

Elsie shook her head furiously. "What if someone finds me? I'll be cast out, with no hope of a reference."

"No one will find you," Grace reassured her. Still, Elsie remained unconvinced. Grace sweetened the offer. "You can drink my chocolate and eat the toast. Would you not enjoy a chance to put your feet up for an hour or so?"

Elsie's gaze drifted toward the tray. "Where will you go?"

"To visit Rol– Lord Percy," Grace replied, catching herself before she uttered his first name without his title. It was quickly becoming a habit, one that was likely to land her in hot water if she said it in front of anyone else.

Of course, Elsie caught the error. The mulish set to her face softened, and a grin tugged at her lips. "You want to visit his lordship? On your own?"

"His man Thorne will be there, I am certain." Grace put her hands on her hips. "I saw something unusual yesterday at the charity bazaar. Roland must be made aware, and he may require my assistance with the matter. It is best if I go and explain myself."

Elsie again eyed the tray. "I will do it, but I am not giving you my clothes. Wait here for a moment, and I will fetch you a set from below stairs."

Elsie returned faster than Grace expected. She helped Grace pull the coarse black dress over her head and tie on the white apron. A simple white cap covered Grace's hair adequately enough. With the addition of a white shawl, Grace felt certain she could hide her face enough to prevent anyone from recognising her.

It felt decidedly odd to use the back staircase, but Grace could hardly swan through the house dressed as a servant. At the foot of the stairs, Grace heard the chattering voices and banging pots echoing from the kitchen. She turned the opposite way, hurrying past the closed doors to the laundry room and storage cupboards. At any other time of day, she would have run a greater risk of discovery on her way out. But this early, the staff was busy preparing the house for the day. Drapes had to be pulled, rooms aired out, and tables prepared before the master and mistress of the house made their appearance.

None of the stableboys paid Grace the least mind when she strode past them, her gaze firmly fixed on the ground. Beyond the stone wall circling their grounds, early morning London unfolded into a tapestry the likes of which she had never seen before. The first thing she noticed was the fresh air carrying the faint scent of bread straight from the oven. Dew sparkled on the grass and leaves. A cart trundled past with its bottles of milk clanking an uneven melody.

Servants and workers hurried past as they rushed about their duties. Grace entertained herself by making guesses as to where they were off. One she determined to be a shopkeeper, another a laundress. A still-drunk upper-class man with his cravat hung loose about his neck and his dishevelled hair made her laugh. There was little risk of him recognising her, giving his halting steps and bleary gaze.

The distance from her home to Roland's was not far. It took her ten minutes of walking at a steady clip to locate his address. How would he react to finding her on his doorstep? His interest in speaking with her had been clear enough the night of the royal event. Surely he would welcome her presence now, especially given the circumstances. Grace tamped down a twinge of worry until it disappeared from her mind.

She spied the front doorstep and nearly ambled up to it before remembering how she was dressed. Servants entered through the rear of the house. She bit her lip and pondered how to handle the task before recalling the presence of the children. The Sprouts, as Elsie had called them.

She circled around and approached the house from behind. When she reached the stables, she peered inside and called a quiet yoo-hoo. A rustle confirmed someone was there, but no one answered. She tried again. "Sprouts? Children?"

A mop top head shot up from inside the nearest empty stall. "Cor! Wes, it's the lady!"

Down the way, another head popped up beside the lone stabled horse. The child rubbed his eyes as though she were a mirage and not a living person.

"How do you know I am a lady?" she asked, genuinely curious. She motioned for the children to come out of their hiding spots.

"You toffs can no more hide your accents than we can ours," the child named Wes answered. "Besides that, your maid knows our names."

Grace conceded the matter with a gracious nod of her head. "Well played. If you would not mind introducing yourselves, I

*The Ruby Dagger*

might also have a better way to refer to you than as something growing in the vegetable patch."

"I'm Wes," the boy answered. He thumbed at his brother. "That's Will—um, Willa."

Willa stepped clear of the stall, allowing Grace a better view. She nearly choked when she noted the child was wearing a dress and not trousers. Still, she covered her shock with a polite cough into her hand. "It is my pleasure to meet you both. You may call me Lady Grace. Now that we are properly introduced, I must ask a favour. Could one of you let Lord Percy know that I am here?"

Wes pulled a face. "His lordship ain't here, my lady. He took Arion out for a ride."

Grace froze in place. This was not an outcome she had envisioned when making her plans. Should she ask when he was expected to return? Would the children have an answer? Even if they did, she could not afford to wait around. Sooner or later, someone would notice her absence from home. She shifted from side to side, torn whether to stay or go.

"Want us to get Mr Thorne?" the girl offered. "Maybe he can help? Or he could fetch his lordship if you need 'em straight away."

Grace latched onto the offer. "Yes, please, of course," she burbled. "Thorne will know..."

The child dashed off without a backwards glance, arms flapping as she ran across the yard to the kitchen door. Grace laced her fingers together and adopted the poised stance she relied upon at evening balls. It was a position she could hold for hours, appearing perfectly content and not at all in need of an intervention, or a dreaded invitation to dance. Across the stable, the boy eyed her and then shifted his own scrawny limbs as he attempted to copy her pose. If it were not for the determined expression on his face, Grace would have laughed.

83

That was how Thorne found her—with her lips mashed together to keep a giggle from slipping out. Splitting a look between her and Wes, his own lips quirked, but he bowed low. "My lady, how may I be of assistance? I apologise for Lord Percy's absence, but... I do not believe we were expecting you."

"It was a spur-of-the-moment decision to come," Grace explained. Thorne took this news in without even raising an eyebrow, acting as though debutantes dressed as maids came calling on the regular. Nonetheless, Grace felt compelled to offer more. "I had news for Lord Percy about Lord Vaughan."

"He left not long ago and I do not expect him to return for at least an hour, mayhap more. I would be happy to take the message for him... or is there something more you need to add? You must, given your presence rather than a penned note." Thorne glanced back at the house, considering his next move. "Have you broken your fast, my lady? Mrs Archer always prepares more than we can finish. If you do not mind sharing the table with me, that is. Lord Percy often has me sit with him, but you are not at all required to do the same."

Grace was slightly taken aback—entirely by the idea of a man who would one day be duke sitting with his servant—but the idea that Roland would do so did not surprise her at all. She could somehow not envision him lording over a breakfast table alone but for his tea and paper, and she stifled a laugh at the idea.

But her eyes must have twinkled, and Thorne missed little. He cocked an eyebrow at her, and impulsively, she elaborated, though she blushed at the idea of slighting him to his manservant. "I was trying to imagine Lord Percy enjoying a grand breakfast and the paper by himself."

"Then you understand Sir Barbarian well," Thorne said, his teeth showing in the barest trace of unexpected humour. But quickly he cleared his throat and resumed his properly polite pose, concerned he had slipped too far.

"It is all right; I know how close the two of you are. I would not mind your company in the least. It is a kind offer, and one well appreciated, Mr Thorne." Grace fell into step at his side and followed him into the house. He did not take the stone steps leading to the kitchen on the lower floor, but instead directed to a door off the terrace. The door opened to the dining room.

Grace was powerless against her curiosity. Her steps slowed as her gaze roamed the room, taking in the travertine floor, elaborately carved table and chairs, and the few works of art on display. Equally, she noted the absence of a rug under the table, a painting to fill the discoloured gap on the wall, and a pair of empty marble pedestals. Was Roland hurting for funds, and had to sell off heirlooms? It made no sense, yet her mind leapt that way.

Thorne caught the direction of her gaze. "We are in the midst of redecorating, my lady. Lord Percy's tastes are... somewhat different from those of his father."

His grimace filled the gaps in his words expansively. Whatever the previous Earl Percy had preferred in style obviously did not fit with Roland's more austere tastes, especially if he was willing to forego decoration entirely rather than live with choices of the past generation.

Plates of food lined the centre of the table, showing eggs, ham, toast, and even kippers. Grace glanced around again, wondering where the servants might be.

"Our household is still very small. The housekeeper and butler are out at the market. I promise, there is no one else here to recognise you, nor share a word of your visit." He pulled out a chair for her, taking on the role of footman, and then circled the table to sit across from her. "Lord Percy prefers a more informal style of dining. Help yourself to anything you like."

Grace lifted the spoon from the dish of eggs, noting the weight of the silver and the family crest etched into the handle. Despite the casual arrangement, every item had been polished until it gleamed. Grace filled her plate with her favourites while Thorne did the same. He poured her a cup of tea and then they ate.

It should have been strange, as it was as odd for a lady to share a table with a manservant as it was for the earl to do so. Worse yet—she was doing so with a manservant who was not of her household. Somehow, it was not, simply because both Grace and Thorne chose not to acknowledge it as such.

"Have you and Lord Percy had much luck on your end?" she asked the man. "Roland mentioned that someone was looking into the staff and owner of the hunting knife—the former Commander-in-Chief, I think he said?"

"That would be Sir David Green," Thorne told her. "A man worthy of respect, and an able commander." But he shook his head regarding further news on that front. All he had to share was Prinny's threat and the news about Sir Julian Montgomery and the ambassador's feud.

After a few bites, Thorne asked Grace what she had come over to inform them of. Grace told him of seeing Lord Vaughan at the bazaar, and catching him handing over a wrapped parcel after making sure no one was watching.

"Do you think it might have been the gemstones from the ambassador's dagger? It was too small to be the weapon itself."

"We had word he was donating an item, but I agree with you, his behaviour is passing strange. There would be no need for subterfuge. Yet, we should take care not to see shadows behind every door. Lord Vaughan is known as a collector of rarities, not a thief or a fence. If he were responsible for the theft, I doubt he would be so foolish as to pass over the stones at a public event."

*The Ruby Dagger*

"Still, you admit that his actions were not those of a wholly innocent man," Grace countered. "The only way to determine whether there is a shadow is to open the proverbial door, as you put it. Will you and Lord Percy look into the matter?"

Thorne promised they would. Silence again fell over the table.

Grace lifted her teacup, but was slow to sip. She studied the man across from her. His dark hair and bearing reminded her of Roland, but perhaps that was only to be expected after some ten years of working closely and his sitting at the table, dining like a lord. She had seen him take so many roles. Carriage driver, spy, fighter, and now gentleman. Roland had explained that Thorne had served as his batman, but Grace was sure their connection went deeper than that. These men were friends, dear friends. They trusted one another as equals, not as servant and master.

Grace's mind drifted and her gaze softened as she considered what Roland's friendship with Thorne said about him. For a certainty, her brother Felix would never dine with his valet. Of course, Felix had also never stood upon the field of battle with his valet standing guard. She blinked to clear her vision and found Thorne's blue-eyed gaze fixed upon her.

Grace sat her teacup down with a clink and then cleared her throat. "Thank you for the hospitality, Mr Thorne. I should get back. My family will wake soon. I do not want Elsie to get caught covering for me."

Thorne wiped his face with his napkin and pushed back his chair. "The Sprouts and I will walk you back. Lord Percy would not like the idea of you going on your own."

# 12

More than a full day since the confusing encounters at the parade grounds, Roland still didn't feel any closer to eliminating a suspect from the list. Quite the opposite, in fact.

Frustration saw him setting out from his home again atop Arion shortly after noon. He was supposed to pay a call upon Lady Charity today, but the idea of spending even half an hour cloistered in some fussy parlour, struggling for flowery things to say, made him feel like a badger in a trap. So he sent Wes to forward his regrets and promised to call upon her on the morrow instead.

He needed to move. He needed to think things over, and he always felt that thoughts flowed easier from the back of his horse. He let Arion have his head and allowed the horse to walk wherever he was inclined.

The news that he had missed an unexpected visit from Lady Grace had soured his gut. He was nearly jealous that Thorne had the chance to spend a pleasant time breaking his fast with her while he had been out, giving Arion a much

*The Ruby Dagger*

needed gallop. That sentiment passed swiftly when he realised the import of her news.

Lord Vaughan had been rather low on his list of suspects, particularly in light of the animosity between Sir Julian and the ambassador. Even Thorne admitted that someone with his means could very well fence the jewels from the stolen dagger, and without the same suspicion that would be accorded to a servant. If he was not responsible for the killing—and that still seemed unlikely, as Lord Vaughan was a bit of a dandy of a man—it was not out of the realm of possibility he was abetting the sale.

This whole thing was giving him a mighty headache, and he decided abruptly that food should be the next order of business, as it was nearing the dinner hour and he had not yet even broken his own fast.

Looking up, he realised Arion had brought him rather near St James's street. The grand Georgian structure of his club, Whites, was just ahead. He hadn't eaten out much since Mrs Archer had taken up the cooking duties of the townhouse, but he hoped she would forgive him this once. Resolved, he dismounted and was ushered through the heavy wooden door by the doorman.

It was a little late for luncheon and early for dinner, so the attendance at the club was still light, but Roland found himself seated with oysters and a ceramic stein of dark Porter beer in a trice. The malty beer, he was told, would be the perfect accompaniment to the saltiness. Roast chicken would be forthcoming after.

The food was everything promised, and Roland ate with a good appetite. It was only when he finished his Porter that he looked up from his glass and found a profile he had not expected in the room.

"Is that Ambassador Baron Gustaf Albin Lindberg over

there?" he asked the discreet waiter, who had just shown up to take his plate.

The waiter didn't even glance over to confirm. "Yes, that is his lordship, Baron Lindberg. He has been conducting some of his business here."

Doubtless, the ambassador was staying at the home in Mayfair serving as the embassy, but that did not mean it was a convenient place to network with members of the ton. Perhaps Arion's heading had been fortuitous after all. "Thank you," Roland told the waiter. "I believe I shall go pay my respects."

Leaving his table, Roland straightened his jacket and went over to the ambassador's seat. "May I stand you a drink, Your Excellency?"

The ambassador looked up, half cross, but as recognition flickered across his face, it turned to a vague amusement. "I will not say no to another drink if you join me and ease your manner. I face enough English stiffness to fill my evenings. You—are Earl Percy, yes? I remember you from the presentation dinner."

"Yes. I shall be happy to join you for a drink, then, Baron Lindberg, if there is no imposition."

"Of course. There is no imposition," Lindberg said precisely, signalling for the waiter's attention as Roland sat. "Two more Svensk Punsch, if you please."

When the waiter departed, the ambassador's face turned thoughtful. "You got up during the meal. Then, I thought nothing of it, but now I suspect you were off handling this unpleasant business. The Prince Regent has been most expressive about your... investigative talents."

Roland was uncertain how to reply to that surprising news that Prinny had been speaking of him to the ambassador, so he ignored it for the moment. "I was. I hope that otherwise your visit has been going well."

The ambassador slanted a droll look his way and then

*The Ruby Dagger*

checked to ensure that the nearby tables were empty. "If one overlooks that His Royal Highness Prince Carl Johan of Sweden's gift to the Prince Regent has vanished. Twenty-four years I have spent in diplomacy, and now... catastrophe. I beg your forgiveness, but I do not have much heart to speak about the weather or sights."

"You believe then that you will suffer for the theft?" Roland asked him in a low voice.

"Yes. I will certainly be scrutinised, perhaps more. At least they must investigate and be convinced I was not responsible for its loss."

"I will do what I can to aid you and find the thief," Roland promised. "I do not suppose you have any suspicions about which someone may be motivated to steal it?"

"Who can say, Lord Percy? I have been promised that it is not a common servant. Someone who wishes to embarrass your crown? Or perhaps they wish to embarrass mine."

"Someone, perhaps, who has a vendetta against you personally?" Roland hazarded, wondering if perhaps Lindberg might comment on the curious arguments witnessed between him and Sir Julian.

Lindberg's face tightened, but took a breath and nodded. "Perhaps. I do not know. Your efforts, Lord Percy, are appreciated."

Before he could say more, the waiter returned with their drinks, and Roland decided to let the matter drop for a moment. "I do not believe I have had the opportunity to try this before," Roland said, lifting the glass of neatly served amber liquid to his nose to check its bouquet. It was darkly sweet-smelling and earthy.

"Likely, you will not again once I depart. I brought arrack with me, which is the liqueur you are smelling. Then I had to instruct the staff on how to prepare it. I was given to understand that arrack is not common to find in England. Your people tend to prefer rum and brandy for their sweet drinks, so I do not hold much optimism that it will become popular as a trade item."

Roland sipped the liquid and discovered it was as sweet as its aroma. "It has a most intriguing flavour."

That seemed to please the man as Roland took another, longer sip. "Then you have better taste and a more open mind than many of your brethren here among the gentry. Perhaps you should be a diplomat."

"Until recently, I was fighting against Napoleon. An open mind is a useful thing to have," Roland said, spinning his glass slightly.

"Ah," the ambassador said. Something about his tone snagged Roland's attention, and he looked over at Lindberg. The man had somehow grown a little harder. Colder. "Navy? Command?"

Frowning, Roland set down his glass. "No, cavalry. In the Iberian peninsula, most lately. I am sorry, Baron Lindberg. Have I said something to offend you?"

Lindberg relaxed a trifle. "Be at ease. You have done nothing, Lord Percy." There was a little silence as the baron considered what else to say. "I am simply not wholly comfortable around those with a military mindset."

Roland turned that sentence over in his head, seeing an opportunity. "I suppose I should not ask if you enjoyed the parade yesterday, then."

Barking a laugh, Lindberg swallowed the rest of his drink. "No, yesterday was most thoroughly unpleasant, for many reasons." One of those being his discovery of the theft, no doubt. "Were you there then as well, Percy?"

"I was," Roland allowed, and decided to take a risk. "I saw you there, but only from a distance. I think you were conversing with Sir Julian Montgomery."

*The Ruby Dagger*

Lindberg's fingers tightened on the glass, but he controlled his expression. "Yes, he and I are... familiar with one another. We had dealings five years ago."

Roland could not think of how the two men would have met, since he knew Sir Julian was a career military man, but mostly from British soil, as far as he was aware. He tried to keep his tone innocently inquiring. "Is that so? I did not know Sir Julian had ever gone to the continent."

Nodding, Lindberg fingered the rim of his empty glass. "Oh, yes. Before the war."

The continent had not exactly been quiet in the last decades, but Roland could only think of a few wars where Sir Julian may have crossed Lindberg's path. In 1807, Britain had bombarded Copenhagen to prevent Napoleon from being able to seize the Danish fleet. In 1808, the Peninsula War had begun, and Roland and Thorne had found themselves deployed to Spain. But also, that year, war had begun between Sweden and the Russian empire. He was a little vague on the details of that event, beyond that Sweden had defied Napoleon's Continental System. He hazarded another guess. "The Finnish War?"

Baron Lindberg's face held neutral, but there was something as lifeless about his eyes as a corpse. "Forgive me, Lord Percy. I find I cannot have a conversation about such a topic in polite company. But I will say this much, as you are a young man and more familiar with the might of the sword. Know that diplomacy can be as deadly as war."

Clearly, it was a sensitive subject, and Roland desisted immediately, apologising. Baron Lindberg murmured a polite denial of offence, but reached for his pocket watch to check the time. "I enjoyed our drink. Find the ruby dagger, Lord Percy, and no matter shall be paid to the rest."

"Of course, Baron Lindberg. I hope you have a more pleasant day."

The baron nodded, and both got up from their seats. The baron strode out of the first floor dining room with a purpose, and Roland waited a second before he followed. As they headed separately towards the main stair, Roland expected him to descend and go about his business outside of Whites... but instead he headed away from the staircase, towards the card room.

In and of itself, that was no cause for surprise or consternation. What was concerning, however, was that Lord Peregrine Fitzroy appeared to be waiting for the ambassador's arrival.

How strange that the ambassador would be acquainted with someone who had likely still been at Eton the last time Lindberg set foot on British soil, particularly given Fitzroy had not been at the royal dinner.

# 13

Grace did not dare to sneak out of the house two days in a row. After Elsie helped her dress for the day, she declined the offer of a breakfast tray in favour of joining her father in the morning room.

Lord Tilbury was a creature of habit. He rose at the same time every day, ate the same meal for breakfast, and read the same London broadsheet while finishing his second cup of coffee. On this particular morning, he was still enjoying his fried eggs and buttered toast. He evinced little surprise at his daughter's entry into the room, pausing only long enough to tell her good morning.

"Have you any plans for the day?" he asked in between bites.

"I am sure I do, but Mama has not yet deigned to share them," Grace replied. The footman placed a covered plate before her and removed the silver lid to reveal a sugar-dusted pastry beside a serving of scrambled eggs. He moved along to remove Lord Tilbury's now empty plate. He no sooner left the room through a side door than the family butler arrived, bearing a perfectly pressed newspaper on a silver tray.

"Today's news, my lord."

Something about the butler's tone caught Grace's attention. She rested her fork on her plate and looked at her father. He took the paper and unfolded it to peruse the front-page headlines.

"Upon my word!" Lord Tilbury gasped. His fingers tightened around the edge of the paper and his hands shook the pages. "Can this possibly be? Of all the ghastly risks!"

Grace glanced at the butler, once again standing off to the side, but his impassive features gave her no hint as to the cause of her father's exclamations.

"Regent or not, his behaviour is beyond the pale..." Lord Tilbury switched to muttering under his breath as he read the news.

Grace dared not lift her fork, nor raise her cup for a sip of chocolate. Obviously, something serious had happened overnight. If she asked flat out, or rose from her chair, her father would fold the paper away and take his leave, muttering about things being unsuitable for a young woman. However, if she sat still, and he forgot she was there, she had only to wait until he opened the paper to read the front page.

Her father reread the article in question, stretching out the wait until Grace abandoned all discretion and hurried over beside him. The large, black letters fairly leapt from the page.

*"Gambling Hell Turns Firestorm: Royals Flee for Their Lives!"*

Grace leaned over her father's shoulder to read the smaller print. Her movement caught his eye, and he folded the paper over to prevent her from seeing any more of the dreadful news. "I say, Grace, should you not be in your chair? What if your mama comes in?"

Grace stood her ground. "Mama is still abed, as you well

*The Ruby Dagger*

know. Come now, Papa, what does the article say? What has Prinny done now?"

Her father harrumphed and waved her back to her seat. But, once she displayed the proper decorum, he relented enough to tell her the news. "The Prince Regent and his brother were out carousing and nearly got themselves killed."

He got no further than that. A footman entered the room and carried a message to Lord Tilbury. He waited while his master read the note. Lord Tilbury's brow scrunched as he eyed the seal. He lifted his bread knife and slit open the envelope. His eyes skimmed the page, and he glanced at Grace. "You are invited to the palace."

"For an event?"

"Summoned, I should have said. Without delay." He slid the paper back into the envelope. "Why, dear daughter of mine, is our beloved queen demanding your presence at this hour?"

Grace weighed possible responses before landing upon a version of the truth. "I am assisting her with a small matter. Trivial, really. Who are we to question the queen's desires?" She pushed back her chair and stood. "I should get my jacket and gloves. I am sure you are busy with more important matters, and Mama does so hate to rush. Elsie can accompany me for the ride."

Grace swished her skirts and exited the room with all haste, not giving her father time to stop her. It was a tactic she had learned from her mother. Although Lord Tilbury was the nominal head of the household, Lady Tilbury had perfected ways to ensure she achieved her desired outcomes.

Elsie was still in Grace's room, tidying. She leapt at the chance to accompany Grace to St James's Palace. In short order, the two young women sat in the family carriage as it clattered over the cobblestone streets of Mayfair. A guard waved them through the palace gates. Another helped Grace down from the carriage. She turned back to tell Elsie to wait there when she heard someone say her name.

"Lady Grace," Roland called. He pulled on the reins to draw his horse to a stop and then swung down to the ground. He passed the reins to a waiting stableboy and strode to where Grace stood waiting. "I see the queen sent for you as well. Have you heard the news?"

"Of the Prince Regent? Indeed, I have. We best not keep her waiting."

Roland offered Grace his arm. Together, they walked through the open door into the palace proper. A footman preceded them, guiding them through the corridors along the same route they had taken on the night of the royal event. With her hand resting on Roland's arm, Grace could almost imagine they were there for another special event, perhaps a ball or ceremony. What would it be like to enter such an event with Roland at her side?

Grace dared to cast a glance his way. Her eyes traced the familiar lines of his profile. Sensing her gaze upon his face, he turned his head, his dark eyes meeting her hazel ones. He laid his free hand upon hers and squeezed it, showing his support. Whether that was in preparation for the conversation with the queen, or because he sensed where her mind had gone, Grace did not know.

The footman led them to the throne room. There was no sign of the crime five days earlier, though the queen bore the same forbidding expression. This time it was she who sat upon the throne, while Prinny paced in front of her. The Prince Regent glanced over when Grace and Roland walked through the door.

The man was a far cry from how he had appeared on the night of the dinner. Dark shadows marred his face. Although his clothing was fresh and clean, still bearing the carefully pressed

*The Ruby Dagger*

creases, his hair was in complete disarray. When he stopped in his tracks and spun around to face them, and then ran his fingers through his hair, Grace understood why it was a mess.

"This is your fault," Prinny snarled at the pair. "Your failure to apprehend the thief has now put my life at risk."

Roland jerked to a halt and planted his feet in a wide stance. "I beg your pardon, your highness, but I am unsure what you mean. Has something else been stolen?"

The headline popped into Grace's mind, but like Roland, she could not make a connection between it and the palace incident.

Prinny clenched his hand into a fist and waved it at Roland. "Are you blind and deaf, man? Every broadsheet and newsboy in London is peddling the news of my brush with death."

Roland paused, his eyes flickering beneath his lids, as he again tried to understand what may have happened. "I do not mean to belittle the incident, serious as it must have been, but such things happen in the slums, your highness." Roland said in a carefully moderated tone. "What I do not understand is how you believe it is connected with the events of the state dinner."

"Such things happen?" Prinny rocked back a step, aghast at Roland's response. He turned to face his mother. "*This* is who you trusted to retrieve the stolen dagger?"

Though Prinny reigned over the country, Queen Charlotte was still his mother. She bestowed a fierce glare on her son's angry face. "Lord Percy has a point, dear son, as I have warned you many times before. He may do a better job of connecting these incidents if you share with him what the runners learned."

Prinny folded under his mother's chastisement, although not entirely willingly. He ceased his posturing and ventured over to sit beside the queen in the elegantly carved wooden chair usually reserved for the ruler's consort. He slumped in the chair and then hunched over to rest his head in his hands.

Roland and Grace took this as an invitation to come closer. They crossed the floor of the throne room and took up position at the base of the raised dais upon which sat the throne. Roland released Grace's arm, and she sank into a deep curtsy, not rising until the queen gave them permission.

Grace kept her gaze firmly fixed on the space in between the queen and Prinny, mostly because she was not sure which one of them was more important at that moment. When Prinny raised his head, she shifted her gaze his way.

"We ventured to the Scarlet Jack last night—Frederick and I, that is. It was a common enough occurrence, and hardly worth taking note. The evening proceeded as it usually did. Cards, dice, and, err, other activities." Prinny swallowed. "I was at the tables when the scent of smoke caught my attention. I waved for a guard to check what was wrong. He opened the door to the back of the house and smoke billowed into the gambling room. All hell broke out, then.

"The guard rushed back to my side and tugged me to my feet. He did not even give me time to collect my winnings. Another did the same with Frederick. We were half foxed and trundled along. To be honest, I did not realise the nature of the fire until we made it outside. The roof was red with flames so hot that it glowed beneath the roils of smoke. The guards pushed us further away, urging us toward our carriage. They did not let up until the horses leapt forward to take us to safety."

"Thank heavens for that," the queen muttered darkly. "I fair tremble at the thought of how close I came to losing you and your brother. Tell them about the culprit."

"They caught the man?" Roland asked. "So quickly?"

Prinny nodded his head. "The villain was a fool. He spilled kerosene on his trousers and they caught fire. The guard spotted him lying on the ground near the rear of the building and rushed to his aid, not realising the man was the arsonist until he

*The Ruby Dagger*

got closer. Though the guard tried valiantly to save him, the man was too far gone. He managed to utter only a single phrase."

"What?" Grace asked, unable to stop the word from tumbling from her lips.

Prinny's expression darkened. "He said he was ordered to set the fire that night."

Prinny lapsed into silence, seemingly out of words. Or perhaps the seriousness of the threat finally caught hold. Queen Charlotte softened enough to reach over and pat his arm, almost as though she needed to reassure herself he was there, safe and whole.

Roland waited for the queen's attention to turn back to them. "Has the royal guard been informed?"

"Indeed, they have. We will take care, but we cannot disappear entirely from society, Lord Percy." The queen's gaze shifted from Roland to Grace and back again. "Your progress on this matter is too slow. Where is the dagger? Who is behind this?"

"We have a short list of suspects, your highness. With your permission, we can compare the names with those who may have known your plans to visit the Scarlet Jack last night."

"I will have a list of names sent round later today, after I have spoken with Frederick," Prinny promised. "I expect regular updates, Lord Percy."

"And from you, Lady Grace," the queen added, fixing Grace in her sights. "There is much more than the crown's reputation at stake. I trust you understand the implications of failure."

With that, the royals dismissed Grace and Roland. The pair eased out of the room, taking care not to show the crown any disrespect by turning their back. They did not breathe easily until they were back in the corridor.

The hallway was as empty as it had been on the night

Roland had found Grace staring up at the statue. Then, she had been terrified of someone coming across them together. Now, she was grateful for a moment alone. Even the footman who had shown them in had made himself scarce.

Grace swung around to face Roland. "We must put our heads together and discuss everything we know. Send me a note as soon as you get the list from the Prince Regent. I will figure out a way to come to you."

Roland's brows drew together. "You must not take such a risk."

Grace scoffed. "It is no risk at all. I got away with no one the wiser yesterday, and it was broad daylight. I can do it again, easily."

"Grace, no," Roland said, interrupting her. When she opened her mouth to speak again, he wrapped his hand around her upper arm, forcing her to pay attention to his warnings. "Someone is willing to threaten the crown and Prinny has already told others I am looking into things. If the thief decides I am a threat, there is a risk you might stumble into their field of view."

That stilled her protests. He was right, and there were more risks than he had named. Even being caught sneaking out by her parents would have consequences. But what made her stomach drop was the thought that someone might try to silence him for asking too many questions. Could it truly be so dangerous?

"Am I expected to stand idle while you court all the risk? While you go off on your own?" she asked him.

The corner of his lips turned up slightly, but his voice dropped lower as he murmured, "Thorne and I can take care of a threat to our household. You cannot. I would feel terrible if something happened to you because of me."

He had shifted forward, a bare half inch, and Grace's breath caught within her breast. Was there more feeling there than just

*The Ruby Dagger*

duty to a young woman's safety? Grace stared deep into his eyes, trying to read the thoughts behind them. They were as dark and enigmatic as a forest pool beneath a moonless sky. She tilted her head up and studied him through her lashes.

The bang of a door closing went off like a cannon. Heavy footsteps echoed along the corridor. Roland jerked back as though stung and turned away to see who was coming. The tall hat and red coat proclaimed the new arrival as a member of the guards.

"Go home, Grace. I will finish here and then I must hurry to meet Lady Charity." Roland marched off, raising a hand to hail the approaching guard. He fell into step and walked away, disappearing around the corner.

Grace blinked to clear her vision. She was a silly girl who had read too many romance tales. Of course, Roland cared for her safety more than he would another random girl. They had become friends—of a sort—this season.

But there was nothing more. No matter how fanciful her thoughts got, there could be nothing between them. He knew where his duty was, and it would be best if she remembered that as well.

# 14

Roland much preferred the relative privacy of paying a call to Lady Charity at her house or meeting at Hyde Park. However, the young woman was a savvy sort, and she recognised the importance of being seen in public together. So he did not argue when she suggested Gunter's as their next outing. He owed it to her to put a good face upon their engagement for the sake of her reputation, and since such details did not much matter to him, he generally let her have her way of things.

Confectionary shops were a luxury that Roland had not indulged in. To be fair, it had not seemed to be a wise expenditure of his severely limited funds until after the banns had informed his grandfather of the headway in complying with his decree to marry and set about gaining the next Percy heir. Once he had, his grandfather, appropriately, had expanded his allowance to allow for the courtship and handling of important matters, so it was with some curiosity that he entered Gunter's and let himself be assailed by the unexpected bouquet of flowers, citrus, and spice.

"Have you never been here?" Lady Charity asked him with a charming smile.

"I have not," he admitted, and he attempted to return the smile, but it felt like it did not fit on his face properly. He let it drop after the briefest of moments. She was such a lovely young lady. Kind. Genteel. She would make the perfect duchess.

Why was he not happy?

When he had first determined to marry a diamond of the first water earlier in the season, Lady Charity had seemed to be everything he had wanted in a bride. Roland could not fathom what had changed between the two of them. Why was he not strutting like the other engaged gentlemen, taking pride in winning the lady of his choice?

He had a firm conviction that he would not hold Lady Fitzroy's actions against her. Surely, he was not so cruel. Surely. He must try harder to be a gentleman worthy of her. So he focused on his manners and his courtship, seating her at a table by the window and ordering her a lemon ice. As he was uncertain what to try for himself, he allowed the proprietor to suggest the bergamot.

They took their first few bites, and Roland allowed the ice to melt on his tongue, exploring the curiosity of the experience. "It is... interesting."

"Do you not care for it?" she asked him, and Roland pondered how to phrase his reply politely.

"Actually, it is quite refreshing, but I am uncertain about the bergamot. Perhaps next time I will try a different flavour."

"That is fair," she graciously allowed. "I do not care for the flower ices—lemon is my favourite of all the ones I have tried."

The importance was spectacle. Both Thorne and Lady Charity had explained it to him. They needed to be seen. It was more than just her reputation at stake, Thorne had told him. All members of the gentry made such displays so that others could see them displaying their wealth and standing. Roland could not fathom why anyone should care about flaunting their status in this manner, but he appeared to be in the minority.

"Lord Percy, I wanted to ask you about the guest list," Lady Charity began without preamble. "How many people would you like to invite to our wedding? It would give my mama and me some idea for planning."

His stomach felt cold. Perhaps it was because of the confectionery. "I confess, I do not have many people to invite. My grandfather, the duke, must come, of course." He did not need to explain why his parents would not be present. Lady Charity knew almost as much as anybody could about every member of the ton. "I do not have anyone else."

"Surely there are family friends in London you would want to invite," she encouraged.

If he could invite a friendly face, it would be Thorne. But even he knew that would not be appropriate. He looked down at his ice, making small patterns with the tip of his spoon. "Acquaintances, mostly. The closest thing I had to a friend among the ton was Lord Fitzroy, and I would not be so rude to you."

A faint wash of colour bloomed on her cheeks, but she held her face so composed that he could not determine the feeling that prompted it. She, too, looked away, her eyes growing distant with thought. "I think then we should have a very small, private wedding at the church, but we can have a grander party after."

"If that is what you like," Roland murmured.

Lady Charity touched his hand briefly, forcing him to meet her steady blue gaze. She gave him a look that was filled with compassion. "Perhaps most importantly, though, we should set a date. When would be appropriate?"

Her perfectly reasonable question made the world spin, and Roland held himself stock still while the dizziness passed,

*The Ruby Dagger*

grasping for an answer. "I am not sure," he finally answered. Too brief. He cast around for something else to say. "I am sorry, Lady Charity, I am not very good at this sort of thing. I do not know when the good months of the year are to host such events, or who should be invited beyond my grandfather. Perhaps it would be best if you choose whatever makes you happy or serves the best purpose. I trust you implicitly in knowing the ways of the ton."

"It is your wedding too, Lord Percy. I want you to have a say in what makes you happy as well."

He could not meet her eyes, but he knew she was being heartfelt. "You are as generous as you are kind, Lady Charity. Whatever makes you happy will satisfy me."

"I do not suppose you would like to express a preference in colours or flowers?" she asked hopefully.

His tongue tied itself in knots. He could not even come up with more than a couple of flower names. "...Roses are nice," he finally ventured. "Whatever colour they come in."

Lady Charity was silent for a moment, and he sensed, more than saw, that she turned her head to gaze speculatively out the window, letting the remaining half of her ice melt in the cup untouched. "You are still preoccupied with thoughts of the state dinner, then?" she asked softly, not wanting to be overheard.

Roland nodded briefly. "So far, it does not go well. We have not been able to narrow down any of the suspects."

"Do you believe that the attack mentioned in the papers had aught to do with it?"

Finally, Roland looked up from his cup to her again, seeing no disappointment or frustration with him, only an honest query. "It does," he admitted quietly, for such details had not been included in the paper. "The queen and Prinny confirmed as much to us this morning, so the matter is only more dangerous and desperate now."

Lady Charity bit the edge of her lip, a small crease forming between her brows. "Is there danger to you and Grace in this investigation?"

How quickly she landed on the same point of worry that he did. Briefly, he ran his hand through his hair. "I fear the possibility. Not that I am worried half so much for myself as for Lady Grace. She is acutely vulnerable if someone should take hostile actions against her."

She nodded her agreement. "Then perhaps we would be best served talking about this rather than the fripperies of a wedding?" she offered, and Roland finally allowed a small but genuine smile to come to his lips.

"I am sorry. It is not much of a romantic topic."

She lifted one shoulder in dismissal of that consideration, her pose studiously untroubled. "At least on this matter, we are able to find a common ground. What were you told of the events that happened to Prinny?"

Roland briefly relayed the highlights of the tale, what parts of it he deemed safe for Charity's ears. He ended with the news of the dying man's final words. "Someone else's hand is at work here."

Pressing her lips together in thought, Lady Charity considered this. "If someone had sent the man to the gambling hell with the task, then it follows that someone knew they would find Prinny there. Who would have such information?"

Drumming his fingers briefly on the table, Roland rattled off the woefully short list. "His guards and closest servants, likely, which does not do much to help point to a culprit."

"If they were bribed to provide such information, then perhaps not. However, I can think of a far simpler way to follow his movements. Prinny's wilder antics are hardly secret, and he never ventures out alone. I cannot imagine that was the first time he frequented the place. He must be known to the other

*The Ruby Dagger*

patrons," she pointed out. "Could a patron not have let slip this habit of his? If so, your villain had only to keep watch to catch him there."

Mulling that over, Roland's mouth twisted into a grimace. "I forget how cut-throat high society can be. At least on the field of battle, you know to watch your back. You are correct. It would be much easier to set spies upon the gambling hell than to bribe a guard. Yet, Prinny's visits to such a place do not usually make the papers. The question now is, which of our possible suspects share his penchant for gambling in the slums?"

"On this, I cannot help," Lady Charity said ruefully. "My past suitors told many tales of their pastimes, but visiting such places was not among them."

"No, of course not." Roland's neck grew hot in embarrassment. What was he thinking to pose such a question to Lady Charity? "I beg your pardon, Lady Charity, for how far this conversation has drifted. I will attempt to limit myself to more appropriate matters the next time we are together."

"Perhaps we might discuss our plans for after the wedding? There is the matter of a honeymoon, and then we should decide where to spend the winter."

"The winter?" Roland repeated. Memories of his childhood flashed before his eyes. His parents retreated to their country house, each finding ways to occupy their time so as to cross paths as little as possible. He was certain Lady Charity would be happier without him underfoot. He would do his duty and then grant her the freedom of going wherever she liked. "I have not been to our country estate in years, but I am sure it has been well kept in my absence. You may consider it yours to decorate as you like."

"And what of your preferences, Lord Percy?"

Roland's only preference was to avoid the fate of his parent's miserable marriage. "If you are happy, so am I."

Charity waited a moment, perhaps expecting him to say something more. When he remained mum, she slid her gloves back on and glanced out the window. "I must take my leave. My mama—she's standing there outside the window even now, and she will charge in if I do not show myself out soon. If I am not mistaken, that is Lord Fitzroy, off in the distance. I would think a young gentleman of his age, and... well. Even before everything, he had a reputation for high spirits and questionable activities. I think he stands a good chance of being acquainted with a gambling hell... or at least, who might frequent one."

"That is an excellent suggestion. Until next time, Lady Charity," he replied. And because he could indeed see several people watching them covertly outside the window, he took her hand, bowing over it. "Farewell."

He waited for a moment, watching as Lady Charity joined her mother and began to walk away. Taking a gamble, he headed in the direction of the square nearby where many members of the ton congregated beneath the shade of the trees to ward off the growing heat. Lord Fitzroy's pale blond hair indeed was among them, although the man stood in an odd bubble of space not of his own making. It seemed that perhaps Grace was correct; there was a subtle ostracism of the Fitzroy family happening.

Peregrine saw him coming, and raised an eyebrow in a jaunty greeting, daring Roland to approach the outcast. Naturally, Roland could not care less about what the ton would believe of their meeting.

"How fare you today, Fitzroy?" Roland began without preamble.

"Ah, Lord Percy. As you can see, I am doing well." His voice was light, but somewhat mocking, and his gesture indicated the people nearby who were whispering about the two of them together. "But you may not wish to stain your clothing, talking

*The Ruby Dagger*

to me. My mother's position at the table this past week has been all most anyone can speak of, and everyone has been delicately asking what she did to earn it."

Clasping his hands in front of him, Roland ignored the gossips. "I saw you at Whites yesterday evening. I would have spoken with you, but you were busy with the ambassador."

"Ah. Yes." Fitzroy made a face, but did not expand on it.

Lowering his voice, Roland leaned forward slightly. "Peregrine, I do not hold you responsible for the doings of your mother. I do believe you had no idea."

Candidly, Fitzroy studied Roland, and nodded once. "Then you are perhaps the only one who feels so—among those who know. My lady mother is hard at work at the task of repairing the damage between herself and the queen. You may have heard of her philanthropic efforts at the bazaar."

"I take it that it is not going well."

Waving his hand in negation, Fitzroy paused, considering his words. "She has her work cut out for her. Truly, I believe her when she said she did not intend for any physical harm to come to Lady Charity. But... I am considering travelling abroad for a spell, while matters settle. There may be some business opportunities there that I might take advantage of as an excuse to be away. I decided to pick the ambassador's thoughts about Stockholm."

It was certainly a legitimate excuse to talk to the man. "I see," Roland said. "If you decide to go, I wish you luck in your business endeavours."

"My thanks," Fitzroy replied, tipping his hat slightly in a manner that was vaguely sarcastic. "I expect, given your question and the rumours swirling, you are again on the queen's leash. In truth, my mother would have nothing to do with a gambling hell. I expect you know this, yes?"

"I do. I am not here to make an accusation; I only seek

information, Fitzroy. Who among the gentry might be a regular at these establishments? No one has come forward, but perhaps I might be able to find someone who saw something suspicious last night." It was a partial truth, but still, he was curious how Fitzroy would react.

Fitzroy looked contemplative, but not suspicious. "I am not surprised members of the ton would hesitate to admit to an association with a gambling hell. Even Prinny would be loath to gad it about."

"Have you ever been to one?" Roland asked, curious.

"Once or twice in my earlier years–who has not visited one as a young man?—but I have not been to the one that burned down." Fitzroy rubbed his chin. "I am sorry I cannot be more helpful. You may try, however, inquiring with a friend of mine. He is at quits with the gambling, I am given to understand, and that is long overdue if the rumours of his debts were to be believed. But they are all settled now, as far as I know. Given he was the one who brought me to such a den in the first place, he may be able to provide you with some further names for inquiry."

"There is little to lose in inquiring. Thank you, Fitzroy. I will check with him. What is his name?"

"Matthew Green," Fitzroy said. "He was also at Eton, although perhaps he began attending just after you left. He is barely four and twenty."

Roland paused. "Matthew Green. Is he of any relation to Sir David Green?"

"Sir David is his father," Fitzroy said, nodding.

"All right. I will inquire with him to see if he is aware of anyone who patronised The Scarlet Jack."

"Farewell, Percy. And congratulations on your nuptials."

# 15

Grace stared across the room at her writing desk. She had spent the entire day paying calls with her mother, hoping to learn something of value, but had naught to report back to Roland.

Lord Percy, she corrected herself. She had to cease thinking of him on such friendly terms. Her cheeks burned at the memory of how close she came to embarrassing herself outside the throne room, mooning over him like a lovesick chit. His parting words had fallen upon her like well water, dousing her imaginings of feelings towards her and bringing her back to earth.

She hadn't even planned to seriously consider courting this season—presenting herself had been nothing more than the means to escaping the country estate. Still, she thought privately, perhaps marriage was not such a terrible prospect. At least, it might not be if she could find another like Percy. But what were the odds of that? She sighed and pictured his face again, his chocolate eyes as deep, rich, and enticing as her morning beverage on a cold winter's day.

"My lady?" Elsie called from the dressing room, putting a

hard stop to Grace's flight of fancy. "Do you want me to select a dress for today?"

Grace rose from her chair and ambled to the room next door. The heady scents of lavender and herbs filled the air, clearing her mind of all but her current responsibilities. She was to accompany her family to a garden party at the Arlington home. She let her fingertips skim along the rows of day dresses hanging there until she settled upon a muslin gown with a long sleeve and a flattering neckline. Elsie retrieved the Pomerian mantle of blue satin and a matching bonnet. Grace returned to her bedroom while Elsie located her favourite pair of kid half-boots and pale blue gloves.

Elsie breezed into the room with the requested items in hand. "Did you want me to carry a message to Mr Thorne today?"

Grace shook her head. "I have little to add that has not already been covered by the press. The behaviour of the Prince Regent was not deemed to be a suitable topic of conversation for debutantes. I had to resort to eavesdropping, but even that yielded nothing."

"Chin up, miss," Elsie said as she helped Grace with her boots. "You're frightfully clever, as is Lord Percy. I'm sure you'll uncover something soon enough."

Grace prayed Elsie was correct.

A rap on the door prevented the conversation from continuing. Lady Tilbury strode in with a determined expression on her face. She came to a halt when she spied Grace, dressed and ready to depart.

"Do my eyes deceive me, or are you prepared a full hour before we are due to leave?"

"I am, Mama," Grace answered. When her mother failed to smile in satisfaction, Grace added, "Is aught wrong? Should I have chosen another dress?"

*The Ruby Dagger*

"No, your clothing is perfectly acceptable. As is your attitude, and that is what has me worried. It is unlike you to abandon your habit of reading the newspaper in favour of getting dressed without me having to prod you. Especially when it happens two days in a row. Which begs the question you have so carefully avoided answering until now. Why did the queen send for you yesterday morning? Please tell me it has nothing to do with Prinny's adventure."

"What would I know of a gambling den, Mama?" Grace replied, carefully sidestepping her mother's question. "As for the queen, she has set a new task for me. Another mystery to solve."

Lady Tilbury's nostrils flared, a sure sign she was unhappy.

Grace held up a hand to stop her before she fired off. "Should I have said no? I thought you would be pleased that the queen regards me with such favour. Have we not benefitted from my efforts to find Lady Charity?"

Lady Tilbury rocked back. "Err, yes, I suppose we have. It is just that this is not what I wanted for your first season, Grace. You should be entertaining suitors and considering your options, not haring about town, poking your nose into matters that do not concern you."

"Can I not do both?" Grace fluttered her lashes most innocently. "If I promise to speak with at least one potential suitor today, will that ease your worries, Mama? Might you have some suggestions of someone with whom my time would be best spent?"

As expected, Lady Tilbury grasped hold of the topic of possible suitors and launched into a list of noblemen who met her criteria. Grace gave every appearance of taking note, although her mind was elsewhere. A familiar name jerked Grace back to the present.

"Did you say Montgomery?" Grace asked her mother.

"Yes, and I knew you were no longer paying attention. Why bother to ask for my aid if you let your mind wander elsewhere? I swear, we will never find a husband for you if you do not make even the least amount of effort."

Grace was paying attention now, although not for the reason her mother wanted. "Sir Julian Montgomery? Does he not have a wife?"

Lady Tilbury heaved a sigh of frustration. "Yes, Grace. He has a wife and three sons, two of whom would make excellent prospects for you. They have been away on their grand tour, and I am not certain when they are expected to return. You might ask the man, should you cross paths with him today. Tell him Felix mentioned them, if you must. We would not want you to be seen as forward."

"Of course not," Grace agreed.

Another rap on the door caught Grace and her mother off guard. Lady Tilbury bade the person to come in. Ross, the new footman, explained they had a visitor. "Lady Charity is here to see Lady Grace. Shall I have her wait in the drawing room?"

"Send her up here," Grace answered before her mother could say otherwise. After the footman departed, Grace explained, "Charity is most knowledgeable about this season's suitors. She promised to come round and offer her advice."

Charity had done no such thing. In fact, Grace had no idea why Charity was there, but she was not about to admit that to her mother. What if Charity came bearing a message from Roland? Grace did not want her mother to overhear.

"Charity has done quite well for herself, difficulties notwithstanding. You two may put your heads together until it is time for us to depart." Lady Tilbury stopped when the door opened and Charity came in. "Good afternoon, Lady Charity. I assume your family will attend the Arlingtons' party."

Charity bobbed a curtsy before saying hello. "Yes, Lady

*The Ruby Dagger*

Tilbury. My mama said I might ride over in your carriage, if that is acceptable."

"We have plenty of space! It is only Grace and myself today. I will have Ross run a note over to confirm." Lady Tilbury cast a narrow-eyed glance at Grace before leaving. Elsie followed suit, and the young women found themselves alone.

Charity's expression crumbled as she sank onto the settee near the fireplace. "Grace, I need your advice."

Grace nearly stumbled at the strange words falling from Charity's lips. Their meaning was clear enough, however, Charity had never before uttered that particular combination to her. "From me? My advice?"

"You are the only one I trust," Charity said. She pointed toward the chair next to hers and begged Grace to sit. "I am in a quandary, Grace."

Grace settled into the seat and shifted until she faced Charity. She studied her friend's face, searching for some hint as to the cause of her distress. Her coiffure had nary a stray strand, and her gown was of the latest cut. Yet, Grace could not miss the faint blue shadows beneath her dearest friend's eyes. Her mind skipped back to their last chat together in the garden, and Charity's mention of the cold shoulders some of society tossed her way.

"If someone is giving you problems," Grace muttered, her temper rising. "Has someone said something to you? About you?"

"You know the answer to that, but that is not why I am here. It is Lord Percy."

Grace reared back. "Ro– Lord Percy? What? Why?"

Charity forced her posture to straighten, though she kept her gaze on her hands. Her fingers twisted together where they rested on her lap. She took a deep breath, as though fortifying herself for a difficult topic.

Grace held perfectly still. Had Roland said something to Charity? Had he hinted at Grace's behaviour?

"I do not believe Lord Percy truly wishes to marry me."

Grace blinked several times. "Why would you say that? Did he say something to that effect?"

Charity lifted her gaze. "No, but I cannot help having my doubts."

"Charity, the man searched for you when you went missing!"

"He searched for the diamond," Charity corrected Grace. "He pledged to wed the diamond. When the diamond went missing, he threw his all into finding her. But now I am here, and we are engaged. And... something is amiss. The man makes no effort to get to know me better. He has even less interest in discussing our wedding and the reception. I have long since abandoned any hope of working to plan for what comes after."

Grace's stomach churned with indecision and hope and fear. Until that moment, she had no idea such emotions could coexist. What to say to Charity? She did not wish to cause her friend more pain. However, discussing her forthcoming marriage was not exactly a joyful topic for Grace, even if she did not want to admit it even to herself.

One glance at Charity's face ruled out the option of remaining silent. There was nothing for it but to thread a narrow path.

"Lord Percy is distracted by the queen's latest assignment. I am certain things will change once we uncover the identity of the murderer and retrieve the stolen dagger."

Charity was unconvinced. "Grace, you have spent more time avoiding suitors than speaking with them, so you must trust me when I say his behaviour is unusual. The other men who vied for my hand spoke of country estates, London townhomes, and taking the waters in Bath and Brighton. They offered me a

*The Ruby Dagger*

glimpse of our futures together. Lord Percy has not given me a single hint of what he foresees."

"He has not?" Grace did not know what to make of that.

Charity shook her head. "Every question I ask receives the same answer—whatever makes you happy. What I would like is for him to care enough to form an opinion. He has been to war, commanded troops. He is obviously capable of making a decision, even in the face of great challenge. So why does he not do so now? I spent half the night with that question circling around in my mind. I can only come to one conclusion."

Grace had not a single clue what that conclusion was. "Well, go on then, tell me."

"I—I worry that perhaps Lord Percy's plans to woo someone else were interrupted when you found me after all."

Charity's words hung in the air, suspended like the sword of Damocles over Grace's neck. Grace barely stopped herself from rubbing the back of her neck.

Grace gulped. "I do not follow your logic. Who is this other woman?"

Charity shrugged her shoulders and then tossed her hands in the air. "You tell me? Did he court anyone else while I was indisposed? Was there any young woman who worked to catch his eye? Or mayhap a rumour of a chorus girl... or someone in Spain? He has been abroad for many years. For all we know, he might have a wife and children somewhere else."

Grace was powerless against the froth of giggles that burst forth from her lips. The image of Roland—dutiful and loyal Roland—having two wives and two families was so impossible to imagine. Charity's eyes grew wide as she took in her friend's mirth. She scowled, which only made Grace laugh harder. Eventually, even Charity saw the humour in her statement. It took several minutes and much fanning for the pair to get a hold of themselves.

"Oh Grace, you are so good to put up with me. I suppose you are right. I have let my imagination run away with me. He is not hiding a secret family in Spain." But a darker shadow crossed her face. "If it is not another woman... do you suppose the fault lies with me? You know what some of the ton has been saying about my absence, despite the queen."

She could not fail to comfort her in that. Grace switched to the seat beside Charity and put an arm around her friend's shoulders, feeling an odd frisson of guilt. "Definitely not. Lord Percy is loyal to a fault, Charity. He has a strong sense of responsibility to his country, the crown, and to those who depend on him. He does not want to fail anyone, least of all you."

"Truly, though, there is no one else? He does not consider me damaged goods?"

"No," she answered honestly. Roland lacked much of the gentility of his peers, but perhaps that was not a bad thing. Any other gentleman would have cast Charity off the moment she had disappeared, and Grace could not imagine such cruelty in him. He would be someone else entirely. "If something is amiss with Lord Percy, it is not a fault of yours. He is not much of a social creature. Perhaps he will unbend once you are wed and away from London."

"Perhaps," murmured Charity, but her face looked undecided.

# 16

While it was still within Mayfair and eminently respectable, Mount Street was not quite as grand or prestigious as the area around Grosvenor Square. The Georgian style townhouses were still gracious and desirable, but the people who lived there trended more towards wealthy professionals and retired military than titled nobility. It was close to Hyde Park, and homes in the neighbourhood were far more affordable.

Following his outing with Lady Charity the day before, Roland had written straight to Sir David Green with a request to pay a call to his household. Sir David had written back gladly, inviting him to visit this afternoon.

The brick townhouses around him were clean and well-kept, sash windows framed neatly with panelled shutters. It seemed strange to picture his old commander living in such a sedate neighbourhood. The man had boasted such a forceful presence on the battlefield, yet here, there was nothing to distinguish him from the men living in the houses next door. Was this what the future held for Roland? Could he find satisfaction in the simpler everyday life of the upper class?

Roland could well imagine Thorne's response to such a remark. The man would end up bent over with laughter at the picture of Roland drinking tea and puttering around the house. In many ways, it was for the best that Roland had no intention of settling into married life. Lady Charity would be free to follow her own interests while raising his heirs. He simply had to find a useful way to occupy his own time.

Now, however, was not the time for such thoughts. At Sir David's house, he was escorted inside by a butler who was rather young for the role—the man seemed perhaps mid forties, and his hair still retained much of the colour of its youth.

"Roland," Sir David greeted him, clasping his hand firmly. "It is good to see you again. How goes the investigation?"

"Poorly, to be candid." Roland admitted. "Thorne has been looking into fences, but there has been no trace of the missing diplomatic gift, and the ambassador is beside himself."

Sir David pulled a sympathetic grimace. "Come in. Tell me all about it. Collins, will you fetch us some tea?"

The butler withdrew, and Sir David led Roland into his drawing room, which was kitted with mahogany and deep, hunter green wallpaper. It was small, but quite cosy and well used. Roland settled himself in one of the plush wingbacks clustered conversationally beside the unlit fireplace. It was barely minutes before Collins arrived again with his tray, and soundlessly, the butler poured two cups.

"Only one lump," Roland said, and accepted his cup.

"I am not surprised to learn that you are having difficulty with your investigation," Sir David said, settling heavily in his chair. "You and Thorne are not the only parties who have been set to search for the missing dagger, and some of them are being rather unsubtle about what they are looking for. The number of queries being directed to the fences about 'rubies of the finest carat' and fine gold has the underbelly of London on guard."

*The Ruby Dagger*

Sir David's news made Roland's fingers tighten on the handle of the teacup, and he set it down before he accidentally broke it. "Wonderful. If the thief has heard—"

"And he probably has."

"—he will not attempt to fence the dagger until the matter has been forgotten. Or he may try to fence it elsewhere in a manner more difficult to track."

Sir David made a sound of agreement. "Then... there's the matter of Prinny himself."

It did not surprise him that Prinny was making a muddle of things. "What has he done now?" Roland asked.

"Prinny has set tongues wagging that you are performing some investigation on his behalf. If I heard it, others will. It would take little wit for the culprit to tie this information together. The gossip has cost you any advantage you may have in questioning."

With a breath, Roland closed his eyes in resignation. "What is done is done. I will carry on as best I can. But this may explain much about why certain avenues have not been fruitful."

"Take heart, lad. Not all is lost yet." Sir David drained his cup and set it down. "But my news is not what prompted you to come, yes? Is there something I might do to aid you, or did you call for another reason?"

"I was perhaps wondering if your son was in residence, sir."

"Matthew?" Sir David asked, his bushy eyebrows wrinkling high on his forehead. "What does he have to do with this? He is not involved, is he?"

"No," Roland rushed to reassure his mentor. "I do not believe so. I only seek information he might possess about a certain gambling hell. It may again be another dead end."

Now Sir David's face grew thunderous. "Tell me," he ordered, and then he turned to Collins, demanding that he retrieve Matthew at once.

Roland did not wait for the butler's return before he explained. "I am sure you know—as all of London knows—there was a fire last night at the Scarlet Jack and Prinny was there. What has not been made public is that the fire appears to have been set deliberately to target the Prince Regent."

"To attack Prinny!" David gasped. "But why?"

"If I had the answer to that question, my friend, perhaps I would have a better idea who the culprit is."

There was the sound of footsteps on the stair in the next room, and both men ceased their conversation as Matthew Green joined them in the drawing room. The young man was much as Lord Fitzroy described him, in his early twenties and still lacking the full flesh of adulthood. He had his father's same washed-out blue eyes and a somewhat blonder shade of what had been Sir David's shade in his younger years.

"You requested my presence, father?" Matthew asked, splitting a look between Roland and Sir David.

Both men stood up to include him in their conversation. "Son, meet Lord Percy, one of my former cavalry charges." He grabbed Roland's shoulder in camaraderie. "I trained him when he was naught but a raw recruit at the Salisbury Plain, when we were preparing for Napoleon's invasions."

Roland smiled faintly, remembering the large open spaces where they had practised their manoeuvres before being deployed to Sussex. "Mr Green, it is indeed a pleasure to make your acquaintance. Your father is correct. He had the misfortune of knowing me as a stripling, but he taught me a great deal."

"It is a pleasure to meet you, my lord," Matthew replied. His face, however, indicated it was anything but. "What may I do for you?"

"I was given to understand we have a mutual friend in

*The Ruby Dagger*

common, Mr Green. Lord Peregrine Fitzroy says your times at Eton overlapped," Roland said.

"Yes, that is correct," Matthew confirmed.

"He also says that in the past, you frequented gambling hells together."

Matthew froze then, his gaze crashing into his father's. "Yes, in our younger years, we did. But he and I have not gone together to such places lately. Certainly not at all this season."

Roland wondered why the man seemed so uncomfortable. "Lord Fitzroy was unable to assist me much in the way of this query, but he suggested that you might know... You might be able to indicate who among the gentry frequent gambling establishments?"

"Oh," Matthew said, his forehead easing. "That would be a rather long list, my lord. Perhaps half the men of the ton visit gambling hells, at least occasionally."

"I understand," Roland said, clasping his hands. "I am just trying to find out who attends regularly. With any luck, I might find someone who frequents the Scarlet Jack."

"Just that place?" Matthew asked, tensing somewhat again.

"I do expect it may be a needle in a haystack," Roland acknowledged, spreading his hands. "But any names may help me eventually stumble across the trail of someone who had been there last night before the Scarlet Jack caught ablaze."

Before Matthew could answer, Sir David interrupted. "Matthew may not be able to narrow your search, Roland. He abandoned the gambling tables to better himself. His information may be sorely out of date."

"Actually, father..." Matthew said, clenching his jaw. "I myself was one of those who was at the Scarlet Jack last night."

"You what!" Sir David nearly shouted, rounding on his son.

"At ease, Sir David," Roland said soothingly, trying to calm him.

"I did not gamble," Matthew insisted to his father. "Not much. Just two hands of Whist while I shared a drink with my friends, and I stopped when I was neither richer nor poorer." He turned to Roland. "You are asking about the fire and Prinny, am I correct?"

"I am making some inquiries," Roland acknowledged. "Were you there when Prinny arrived?"

"Yes. I do not know exactly at what time he arrived, but he was playing Roly Poly when I left," Matthew said, scratching the back of his head. "All was fine when I departed."

Sir David's face was grim, but it seemed he was more shocked and dismayed at the news his son was gambling at all than the fact he had been there last night. Perhaps Matthew had had a gambling problem once, Roland thought, reading between the lines of Fitzroy's and Sir David's comments. "What time did you depart? Did you notice anyone suspicious?"

"A little after two. Perhaps fifteen or twenty minutes past? I made an early evening of it," he said, slanting a look at his father. "And no... I do not recall seeing anyone who looked disgruntled enough to set a fire. You think it may have been a sore loser who lost his winnings? That could follow."

The guards had caught the arsonist at roughly a quarter to three and he likely set the fire only ten or fifteen minutes after Matthew's departure.

Sir David's son's departure was timely, if his involvement was coincidental. It was sheer blessedness that kept there from being any fatalities last night at all—although he was given to understand some people had been burned. But Roland did not believe that Matthew would be forthcoming if he had been responsible for any part of the attack.

"Do you recall who may have been leaving at around the same time?" Roland asked Matthew, grasping at straws. "Did your friends also leave at the same time you did?"

*The Ruby Dagger*

Frowning, Matthew looked down at his feet as he recalled the night before. "I was far from the door and could not see who may have departed shortly before I did," he said slowly. "And yes, we all left together; no one else joined us on the way out. But we passed the Roly Poly table on the way out. It was near the exit."

"Yes?" Roland encouraged him. "Did you see anyone you recognised gambling with Prinny?"

"I am sorry, Lord Percy. I do not feel like I am being of much assistance. I do not recall all the faces there, but Lord Sebastian Vaughan was gambling with Prinny for certain."

Roland glanced over at Sir David, whose eyes narrowed thoughtfully as he considered that name his son had provided as well. Sir David knew that Lord Vaughan was one of the handful of names who had left the table.

"You have been more helpful than you think, for if naught else, that gives me another line of inquiry," Roland assured him. "I will not take up more of your time, but I do appreciate your assistance."

Of their short list, Lord Vaughan appeared to be the only one who was present at both incidents. Was it a coincidence? Or had they finally found the trail after all?

# 17

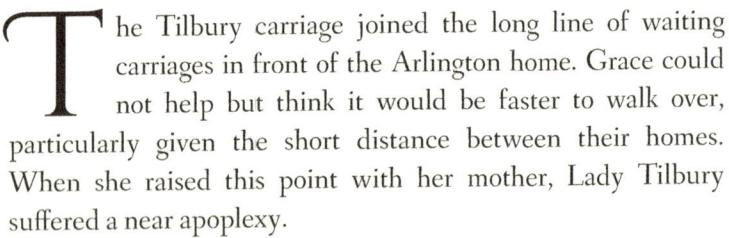

The Tilbury carriage joined the long line of waiting carriages in front of the Arlington home. Grace could not help but think it would be faster to walk over, particularly given the short distance between their homes. When she raised this point with her mother, Lady Tilbury suffered a near apoplexy.

"Ladies of good breeding do not walk to an event unless it is literally next door. The whole of the ton would be speculating we are suffering from money problems, and can no longer afford a driver for our carriage. If you thought your marriage prospects limited now, they would shrivel to none if people thought we could not pay a dowry."

Grace was not sure this was a bad thing, given her lack of interest in being sold off like chattel, but her mother's forbidding expression caused Grace to hold her tongue.

"I am certain Grace merely wanted to stretch her legs, Lady Tilbury," Charity said, intervening before Grace made matters worse. "We spend so many hours indoors, sitting through endless conversations. When the weather is as lovely as today, one cannot help but want to make the most of it."

*The Ruby Dagger*

"Yes, well, I suppose you might have a point there," Lady Tilbury conceded. "But do not get any ideas in your head about wandering off as soon as we arrive. You promised to display your charms today, and I intend to hold you to it."

Grace smiled obediently at her mother, who was sitting across from her on the opposite bench. Then she leaned close to Charity and whispered, "Save yourself, Charity. There is no need for both of us to remain shackled at my mama's leg."

Charity fanned her face to keep from laughing. "I will circulate and see if I can learn anything of value."

At the entrance to the garden, the vibrant sight of lush greenery meticulously shaped into geometric patterns greeted the women. Blooming roses and wisterias added splashes of colour and delicate fragrances that mingled with the fresh scent of cut grass. The soft rustling of leaves and the distant sound of a string quartet set a harmonious backdrop.

Charity spotted her mama across the way and excused herself, leaving Grace with her own mother. Lady Tilbury aimed her steps toward the refreshment tables, where the gentle murmur of conversation, punctuated by light laughter, promised they would find groups of guests conversing. The aroma of freshly prepared refreshments drifted through the air, carrying with it the promise of sweet pastries for Grace to enjoy.

Her mother, however, had no intention of allowing Grace even that bit of freedom. She latched onto Grace's arm and kept a firm hold lest Grace get any thoughts of pulling free. Her first stop was beside Lord Dunstan.

There was much to be said about Lord Dunstan as a potential suitor. He was neither too old nor too young. He had come into his title a few years back and acquitted himself well of the additional responsibilities that came with being the head of the household. His reputation bore no dents, for he was not in the habit of gambling, drinking, or womanising in excess.

If only that was enough to catch Grace's attention! Yet, she found herself wishing he had any unpleasant qualities, for that might make him interesting. As it was, he was a dreadful bore. He was well read and educated, but never veered away from the most bland of discussions. For a woman wanting a staid life with little risk of upset, Lord Dunstan would be an excellent choice. As for Grace, her yearning for adventure stood in diametric opposition to the future Lord Dunstan offered.

She had made this clear to her mama on a number of occasions, but as mamas of the ton were wont to do, Lady Tilbury brushed aside Grace's concerns and continued on.

"Lord Dunstan," Lady Tilbury all but purred, "how delightful to bump into you today."

Lord Dunstan doffed his cap. "Lady Tilbury, Lady Grace, you are as radiant as any of the blossoms in the Arlingtons' garden. It is fine weather, is it not?"

Grace did not roll her eyes at his choice of conversation topic. The weather was a favourite choice among those who had little other opinion to offer. She smiled blithely at the man and let her mother expound upon the topic. That soon proved to be a mistake.

"It is so rare we have an opportunity to enjoy the perfume of flowers and cut grass. Grace was saying earlier today how much she was looking forward to exploring the grounds today. Perhaps you would be willing to escort her around, Lord Dunstan, for you seem well at home here."

Grace gritted her teeth, fully expecting Lord Dunstan to leap at the opportunity. She would have to agree, for she could hardly call her mama a liar.

Lord Dunstan's face flushed, filling his cheeks with a deep stain of red from his nose to his mutton chop sideburns. "I am terribly sorry, Lady Tilbury, but I have already pledged to take Lady Elizabeth for a turn."

*The Ruby Dagger*

As if conjured by her name, Lady Elizabeth stepped out from between a pair of women chatting nearby and scooted close to Lord Dunstan. She threaded her arm through his and fluttered her lashes at Grace and her mother. "Good afternoon, ladies. Have you heard my news?"

"Y*our* news?" Lady Tilbury asked. She could be forgiven for the inflection in her question, for Lady Elizabeth usually imparted news about someone else. Lady Elizabeth, in her third season, had a well-deserved reputation as a bit of a gossip. She always knew the latest on dit and was happy enough to pass it along. She had been quick to bend Grace's ear with regard to Roland and his single-minded determination to wed Lady Charity. For that alone, Grace steered clear of her.

Today, however, she was happy about the interruption. Lady Elizabeth's face shone with happiness, so bright it must not have been feigned. "My father has given Lord Dunstan permission to pay court, and we have been nigh inseparable ever since. Is that not right, my lord?"

Lord Dunstan stood taller and matched Lady Elizabeth's grin with one of his own. "We have yet to find a topic upon which we do not agree."

"Because we are perfectly matched, are we not?" Lady Elizabeth added, finishing his sentences already.

Grace chanced a look at her mother. Lady Tilbury's cheeks were sucked in and her nostrils flared in response to the bitter pill of another suitor gone from the table. And to Lady Elizabeth, no less. The young woman's family name was the only thing opening doors to her now. They certainly could not afford a dowry of any reasonable size. But to someone like Lord Dunstan, with a family name of his own and plenty of wealth to meet his needs, money mattered naught. All he had ever wanted was a woman who would grant him her full attention. After three seasons, Lady Elizabeth had obviously chosen to do just that.

Grace passed along her heartfelt congratulations to the pair and said that if they had any future announcements, they must be sure to share them with her. She did not even have to lie, for she would celebrate the news that Lord Dunstan would no longer be thrust upon her by her mama.

Lady Tilbury gave a pinched smile until the couple were out of earshot. "Look at what you have done, Grace. That girl is nowhere near your level, and yet she has landed a beau."

"After three years of parading herself around at these events, I should hope so," Grace muttered.

Lady Tilbury let her blistering glare serve as a reprimand. "The season is well underway and the most eligible men are being snapped up. Come, let us speak with Lady Anwen. She will have some suggestions of where you should turn next."

Grace followed along without any complaint, for a chat with Lady Anwen would serve her needs as well. The Dowager Duchess of Somerset made Lady Elizabeth's efforts to gossip seem like child's play. She was practically an elder statesman when it came to matters of high society. The only thing she valued more than imparting news was being recognised for her knowledge of such matters.

As was often the case, Lady Anwen sat in the centre of a small seating area on the concrete terrace with two of her granddaughters at her side. She waved them off when she spotted Lady Tilbury coming her way, clearing space for the Tilburys to join her.

Lady Tilbury bobbed a curtsy in front of the older woman. "Well met, your grace. I wonder if you might spare us a moment of your attention."

"I would be delighted," Lady Anwen replied. "My old

*The Ruby Dagger*

bones protest at so much standing, and I oft find myself sitting alone. You will be doing me a favour by taking a seat."

Grace sensed the truth in her statement, for none left Lady Anwen's side without offering some information in trade. She would have to tread carefully to ensure she did not come out the loser, particularly on matters related to the crown.

Lady Tilbury sat in the empty chair on Lady Anwen's right, and Grace took the seat beside her. She preferred to keep her mother as a buffer should the conversation go pear-shaped. Grace noted the excellent view the sitting position offered. Indeed, she could see to the far edge of the garden if she was willing to squint.

The old woman shifted in her chair to keep the sun from shining into her eyes. Once settled, she turned to Lady Tilbury. "Tell me, my dear, how I may be of assistance to you."

"It is my daughter Grace, here. As I am certain you are aware, she put her own quest for a suitor on hold to search for Lady Charity while she was, ahem, away."

Lady Anwen leaned over to get a better look at Grace. "Loyal friend you have proven to be. Yet, I find our queen's idea to hide her diamond away quite strange, for she has never done anything of the sort before. Why did she choose to do such a thing this season?"

The question was directed squarely at Grace, not that she was going to respond with the truth. That was a secret she intended to take to her grave. "Far be it from someone as young and unworldly as I am to question the choices of her highness."

"Harrumph." Lady Anwen huffed at being denied the choicest tidbit of gossip.

"As I was saying," Grace's mama said, "Grace has fallen behind, shall we say, in the hunt for a suitor, through no fault of her own, but you know how such things go. I have encouraged her to wait until she finds someone worthy of her charms, which got us on the topic of young men who are away on their grand tour this year and might be due to return."

Grace added, "Mama mentioned Sir Julian Montgomery's sons, but I profess I do not know the family. What do you advise, your grace? Are they worthy of consideration?"

To Lady Anwen's credit, she did not answer straight away. Instead, she raised her monocle to her right eye and studied Grace. Never before in her life had Grace felt so much like an insect on the pages of Hooke's Micrographia. She resisted the urge to hide her freckles from view.

"The older Montgomery boy is a possibility, but I would not go lower than that," Lady Anwen finally replied, putting Grace out of her misery. "Do you have any hobbies, girl? If not, you will need to find some."

Grace failed to follow the woman's train of thought. "Does the Montgomery family put so much importance on pastimes?"

"Would that they did," Lady Anwen bemoaned. "They are simple people with simple interests. Likely, that is why Sir Julian is so valued by the government as a military advisor and as a negotiator. There is nothing that can be used against him. He does not play cards, barely patronises his club, and does not stray from his vows. I can tell just by looking at you, young lady, that you will not be happy living out quiet days in the countryside."

Grace shuddered at the thought, earning another glare from her mother. "Surely, Sir Julian must be more interesting than that. I heard a rumour that he and the ambassador nearly came to blows at the horse guard parade..."

At this, Lady Anwen shifted position again to lean forward. "I had not heard such, but I confess I am not surprised. They were once rivals, not in love but in war. Sir Julian helped directly negotiate the treaty between Sweden and Britain in 1808. Sweden was promised aid in defying Napoleon's

*The Ruby Dagger*

Continental System, which was strangling the economy. He held tight to the British purse, as were his orders, and what was given was insufficient. Baron Lindburg's son died in the subsequent Finnish war with Russia. My guess is that the baron holds Sir Julian responsible for his loss, even if the blame should go elsewhere. But Sir Julian's face is the one he remembers sitting across the table. I must say, however, that to exchange cross words in public, after all this time, is not seemly."

Lady Tilbury nodded in agreement. "Sir Julian is highly respected by the crown, Grace, even if much of what he has done has been behind the scenes. He is important enough to warrant an invitation to events such as the one at the palace last week."

"Where the man overeats," Lady Anwen said in a low tone. "I misspoke earlier. The man has one vice, albeit harmless to others. At home, his wife carefully controls his meals. When he comes to London on his own, he indulges beyond all limits. I have yet to see him make it through to the end of a meal without having to excuse himself from the table. If you are intent on his son, keep a close eye on whether this vice has been handed down the family line."

Grace fixed her face into a perfectly serious expression and promised to do so. It was a small price to pay for learning why Sir Julian had absented himself from the table for such a long stretch. "Tell me, your grace, what do you know of the ambassador? He must have seen his share of adventures."

# 18

"News from Grace," Thorne told him, handing him the folded paper as they sat at the table together.

The morning ritual of breaking his fast with Thorne in the dining room had started as an inconvenience, but how quickly it had become a part of his day Roland looked forward to. It would be hard to lose this once he married Lady Charity and found her seated across from him instead.

Albert and his wife had already quickly discerned some of his habits, including his distaste for the overindulgence in eating that the members of the ton engaged in, so his standard had become a hearty enough affair, but simple and limited in courses. Today it was potted char with bread and some fresh fruit, with tea. With a grimace, he bit into a piece of the crusty bread, lightly spread with the buttery, flavourful fish. Hopefully, Lady Charity wouldn't also insist on changing his meals to something more elaborate.

"How is she?" he asked Thorne.

Thorne raised an eyebrow over his teacup. "Well enough."

Nodding, Roland spread open her note and reviewed the contents. "Sir Julian is dyspeptic and was indisposed. Well, I

*The Ruby Dagger*

should be happy, I suppose, that we managed to dismiss one name from consideration. Then we are only left with investigating Lord Vaughan."

"He was on the list we received from Prinny, was he not?"

"Yes, he was," Roland confirmed. "Prinny added a note beside his name and mentioned Lord Vaughan has an eye for unusual valuables, including one he would very much like to have back."

"The dagger or something else?"

"He gave no other information, although if he thought for certain the man held the dagger, I doubt he would beat around the bush. What did you learn of the man?"

I have not been able to find much else on him," Thorne admitted. "The lord is constantly in motion, and forever at one event or another I cannot gain access to. It will be up to either you or her to corner him and learn more."

"If I might venture a suggestion—"

Both men looked up, surprised when Albert lifted the teapot and refreshed their drinks. The butler had never ventured an opinion in the middle of their conversations before. As if he realised he had mis-stepped in the most inappropriate fashion, the man stopped and straightened.

"My apologies for interrupting," he demurred.

Roland wiped his mouth hastily. "No, it is quite all right. Please share your thoughts, Albert."

Hesitantly, Albert resumed pouring. "Your home is in need of some decoration. Sotheby's is having an auction this very afternoon."

"You are quite correct," Roland said, nonplussed. "I do need to find time to go shopping but..." he trailed off, not understanding why Albert had brought it up.

Albert looked slightly uncomfortable, but Thorne nodded approval to him. Roland noted with some surprise that the action seemed to steady the man. "Lord Vaughan regularly patronises Sotheby's and is likely to be in attendance if you wish to find him in a neutral place. As an engaged man and an earl furnishing his home, you have sufficient reason to pay your own visit to the auction house."

Understanding lit both Roland's and Thorne's eyes. "Albert," Roland told his butler. "That is an inspired idea. Please, promise me you will interrupt me whenever you have a thought to do so."

"My lord, I shall do no such thing," the butler sniffed, but the older man looked pleased to be thanked so genuinely. "However, I thought perhaps with it just being yourself and Mr Thorne..."

"Yes, of course. However you feel you need to express yourself without breaching propriety—please do so," Roland told him. "I value the trust and input of all the members of my household."

He stood up and both his servants blinked at him. "I need an ink and quill so that I might write a note back to Lady Grace," he explained.

Albert frowned at him and pointed him back to his seat. "You may finish your breakfast, Lord Percy. I shall fetch it."

~

"Father, are you still planning to attend the auction today at Sotheby's?" Grace asked, her face the picture of innocence.

Her father's face flushed. "Yes, I am, but only because that fool owner refuses to see reason. He knows how badly I want that bronze of the lion attacking the horse. I made him a generous offer, but he prefers to line his pocket rather than ensuring it goes to someone who truly values it. I wager few there today will even know who Giambologna is."

*The Ruby Dagger*

Lady Tilbury sat back so the footman could clear her plate. "Why do you ask, Grace? Surely you do not mean to accompany your father."

"Out of the question," Lord Tilbury said, although there was no heat in his words. It was his default response to most anything either of the women suggested.

Grace was undeterred. She had received Roland's latest missive and intended to let nothing stand in her way of making it to the auction. "Sir, surely you can admit I might aid you if I were to come along. A few whispers in the right ears and many a bidder will choose to spend their funds elsewhere. You have only to point me in the right direction."

"Eh?" Lord Tilbury wiped the last crumbs from his beard. "I had not thought it in quite that way."

Lady Tilbury leapt in. "Nor shall you. Grace and I are expecting callers this afternoon."

"Mama, the only people who have promised to come are friends of yours, not mine. You will be able to chat freely without me there to constrain the conversation. And there is the matter of a wedding gift for Charity and Lord Percy. I thought I might have a turn around the auction in case there is something that strikes my fancy. Charity made mention of her desire to update the interiors of the Percy townhouse."

Lady Tilbury's face softened enough to give Grace hope of success. She glanced at her husband. "You will keep an eye on her. Do not let her talk you into bidding on anything inappropriate."

"As if she might!" Lord Tilbury replied, taking umbrage at his wife's suggestion of his weakness. "And do not bring up our village walks as evidence. There is a far cry between buying the child a packet of sweets and allowing her to bid at an auction. Grace, my dear, we must leave promptly at half past two. Ensure you are prepared."

"Of course, Father," Grace promised. Years of practice enabled her to suppress the smile that wanted to cross her face.

She kept up the facade of a dutiful daughter during the carriage ride over by asking her father who might bid against him. Together, they crafted a set of subtle statements he and Grace could let slip to make his opponents have second thoughts. One would cast doubt on the patina, the other would mention wild fluctuations in the market value for such pieces. Together, they felt confident they could winnow away at least those with a casual interest.

Upon arrival, by agreement, Grace and her father split up, Grace heading into the gallery off to the right while her father strode off to say hello to an acquaintance. As soon as Grace was out of sight, she put her mind toward finding Roland.

Grace had accompanied her father to Sotheby's before, so she had some idea of the layout of the space. However, unlike an art gallery, each time she visited, there was something new on display. Today, draped tables and glass cases lined the rooms, allowing bidders to take a closer look at the ancient manuscripts bound in leather, ornate jewellery from the courts of Europe, fine Delft porcelain, and intricate silverwork. She quickly located the Renaissance bronze statue her father coveted, its darkened patina speaking to its age and history. She pretended to study the item before stepping back and shaking her head.

"It's a lovely piece, but it doesn't quite match the patina you'd expect from that era. Could be a later reproduction, though still charming in its own right."

The men standing near glanced at one another and then backed away, taking their interest elsewhere. Grace stayed put, wanting to see what had so enthralled her father. The piece was certainly a showstopper. When Lord Tilbury had first mentioned the title of lion and horse, Grace had foolishly pictured the two beasts standing beside one another. Now, she

*The Ruby Dagger*

recognised how foolish she had been. Instead, the lion had scored great slashes into the side of the horse's flank and was intent on using its fangs to make the killing blow.

"Are we the horse or the lion?" a voice asked. Grace turned to find Roland standing at her side. He cast her a gentle smile. "We hunt for prey, but one false step will see our queen going for our throats."

Grace spoke up to keep that horrid vision from her mind. "Good afternoon, Lord Percy. Fancy meeting you here."

"Indeed," Roland replied. He had his hands tucked behind his back. "Any particular interest in this piece?"

"My father." Grace quieted as another couple drew near. When they stopped to admire the piece, Grace added, "'I heard a similar piece was examined a few years back and turned out to have some serious provenance issues."

"Tough break for the buyer," Roland agreed. He gave her a mischievous grin when the couple moved away. "Was any of that true?"

"Perhaps," was all Grace answered archly, with a small smile. She had spotted Lord Sebastian Vaughan standing on the other side of the room. She nodded his way. "Our prey is within sight, my lord. See that gentleman across the room, in the tailored coat in aquamarine, and voluminous cravat? He is surveying the room with his monocle."

Roland shifted until he could see the man in question. "That is Lord Vaughan, I presume? In that garish monstrosity, he looks more like a Mandarin duck than a man. Have I lost my eyesight, or is he actually wearing a gold waistcoat?"

Her smile grew. "He is. If you would be so kind as to escort me and provide an introduction, I would be happy to inquire about the name of his tailor for you if you would like one of your own."

"Absolutely not," Roland said in mock horror. "But then

again, perhaps you should get that information, if for no other reason than to help me avoid whoever it is." Roland offered Grace his arm and then they meandered in Lord Vaughan's direction.

The dandy's coat colour grew more garish with each step Grace and Roland took. His hair was carefully sculpted, oiled and pomaded until it dared not to move, not even when he shook his head. As he was not studying any of the items on display, Roland walked straight up to him and introduced himself.

"Good afternoon, Lord Vaughan. I hope you do not mind my forwardness in claiming an introduction. Prinny mentioned you might be here and suggested I might impose upon you for some advice."

Lord Vaughan lowered his monocle. "Any friend of Prinny's is a friend of mine, I am sure."

"Excellent. Might I introduce Lady Grace Tilbury? I am Lord Roland Percy."

Lord Vaughan dismissed Grace as the lesser import of the pair and focused his attention on Roland. "Ahh, yes, Lord Percy. I was much aggrieved to learn of your father's passing. He had a true eye for the unusual."

Roland's eye twitched ever so slightly, but he covered it well with a blink. "He did, indeed. Our tastes are somewhat different, one might say. I lack his keen eye."

"That is why you have me here today," Grace said. "I am helping Lord Percy find a wedding gift for his intended bride, my dear friend Lady Charity."

The dandy rocked back on his heels and studied the pair again. "Oh! Pardon me, I thought you two were the ones courting. I see now I was mistaken in my first impression. A bridal gift, how lovely. I am not sure how I can be of aid, though. I know little of the whims of women."

*The Ruby Dagger*

"I had in mind something more unusual." Roland lowered his voice. "His highness said you were the man to meet if I wanted something truly extraordinary. I have heard rumours that your collection includes many rarities, including at least one much coveted by the crown."

Vaughan tossed back his head and sent a booming laugh echoing off the marble floors of the gallery. "I take it Prinny did not tell you what that item is, did he? He would not, for fear of being embarrassed."

Grace's gut tightened in anticipation. Surely Lord Vaughan would not boast of the theft of such a unique and priceless gift to the Prince Regent.

Vaughan shifted forward and lowered his voice until it was barely more than a whisper. "Since Prinny sent you my way, I will let you in on the secret. It serves him right. Perhaps you have heard of our regent's penchant for gambling?"

Roland nodded. "Everyone who reads the broadsheets knows about it. Were you with him the other night when he got into trouble at The Scarlet Jack?"

"Ah, only just. Prinny arrived some thirty minutes or so before I left—before the incident, as luck would have it. Once smoke gets into your clothing, it is nearly impossible to get out. I had on my favourite waistcoat that night."

Grace's impatience grew. "Did the prince wager something he could not afford? Surely the crown has enough money to make good on anything he promised."

Vaughan rubbed his gloved hands together in glee. "It is not money that I desire, young lady, for of that I have plenty. I sought something which money cannot buy..." He went silent, allowing their curiosity to rise to its peak. "An IOU!"

Grace lurched sideways, bumping into Roland's arm. "His vowels? Did he stand them in place of something from the treasury?"

Vaughan shook his head. "It is the promise to grant an unnamed future favour. Tell me now, the both of you, where one might buy a similar item? There is nothing more rare than an unspecified debt from a future king. I shall treasure it forever."

Grace chanced a look at Roland. Based on his wide eyes and half open mouth, he was as gobsmacked as she was.

Lord Vaughan clapped Roland on the back. "You see? Your reaction speaks for itself. That IOU is the most valuable royal item in England right now, I dare say. It is certainly better than anything at the auction. And on that note, I should return to my perusal. I wish you both luck in your bidding. If you want my recommendation, take a look at the Chippendale furniture in the next room. There is a lovely writing desk and chair that your future bride might enjoy."

The man walked off, intent on some other piece up for auction. Grace did not want to stay where she was, where at any moment the fop might turn back and see Roland and Grace lingering where he had left them. She nudged Roland and motioned for him to follow her. Though the distance to the next gallery was short, Grace had time enough to think upon Lord Vaughan's words.

It appeared likely the man did not even know that the ruby dagger was missing. That meant that they had exhausted their list of suspects, and nearly a week on, they were no closer to finding the thief than they had been at the beginning.

The queen would most definitely not be happy.

# 19

As Roland and Grace stood together in front of a Chippendale chair up for auction, the silence lengthened between them, each engrossed in their own thoughts. Finally, Roland stirred himself, realising they might cause whispers if they continued staring at the chair much longer.

"That is that, I suppose. I am out of ideas of where to look. We have run all the leads we had to the ground, and Sir David Green's investigation did not bring any other suspects to the surface," he sighed. "You should—you should probably take your leave of me in case your father sees us together."

Grace looked nearly as despondent as he was, but at his words, she shot him a weakly sympathetic glance. "The wrath of the royal family is what I am concerned about, not the two of us being seen together. If anyone asks, I will repeat the claim that I am helping you pick out a wedding present for Charity."

His heart constricted, and something of the ache must have been reflected in his face, because Grace's disappointment transformed to mild concern. "What is the matter, Roland? Is there some problem you are having between yourself and Charity?"

She called him by his name. Every other time she had done so had mostly been with derision, or anger, or some emotionally fraught moment. He had never heard her use his name this way —as a friend. Someone who cared for his state. That was... it was something he had only ever had with Thorne before.

Hesitating, he indicated that they should move on from this display, and he used the moment to gather his thoughts. "I am sorry," he apologised to her. "I just find myself uneasy with the pace of changes in my life as of late."

Grace nodded, attempting to look serene, but a small line had formed between her brows. It was something she did when she was concentrating very hard, and he wondered if she was aware of it. "You have had a very eventful year," she finally said, "from the very moment you learned of your father's death, your life must have been suddenly overturned."

A rictus of a smile came to his lips unbidden. "You have it exactly. And worse, every moment it seems like I may finally be..." he stopped, grasping for the words. "When I finally discover a place that I fit correctly, something shifts, and everything is upside down again."

They continued walking in silence to the next object on display—some tea set wrought in silver. "I understand, I think," she finally admitted. "I am all too familiar with that sensation of... not quite belonging in a place where I am being put."

Roland looked at Grace and was suddenly reminded of the girl he had twice held in his arms in a dance. A smile came unbidden to his lips at how she had been so rigidly uncomfortable and clumsy. "I suppose you do."

That frown between her eyes deepened with suspicion at his change of mood. "What are you thinking of?"

*The Ruby Dagger*

And that lightened the mood somewhat. "You," he replied. "When I dragged you onto the floor for a waltz." Grace's face went through the most curious range of emotions in an instant—understanding, amused horror... sadness.

It felt private. Wrong somehow, to see her thoughts writ so clearly on her face. He looked away, clearing his throat. "Mostly, I was remembering how... apart from being on the dance floor, you have almost always known exactly who you are and what you wish to pursue in life. I envy you. And that certainty."

"Envy me!" she said with a small scoff. She was stone-still except for letting her fingers wind themselves in her skirts. "Are you saying you are... uncertain about your life?"

Roland pressed his fingertips to his forehead, aware of a headache starting to form. "That's not the right word, exactly, but I cannot find another that makes sense. Perhaps you should just forget I said anything at all."

Abruptly, she changed the conversation in a rush. "Charity... she is afraid that... that you do not truly wish to marry her."

That familiar ache of failure rose in his chest again, and he willed it to subside. "I must have troubled her a great deal if she voiced it aloud to you. It is my fault. I should have paid more attention, pretended more enthusiasm in her planning. I have not meant to be cruel to her."

There was a long pause before she replied. "You would not be cruel on purpose," Grace said, touching his arm for an instant before letting it drop, "but sometimes we are cruel to one another nonetheless when our hearts or plans do not align. Do... you not plan to marry her after all?"

"Of course I will marry her. I harbour no illusion about what a broken engagement would mean in the eyes of the ton, even if the queen would not be personally affronted. I also promised you I would take care of her, Grace." He could hear how his voice grew stilted despite his efforts to remain neutral. "Although you have been vocal in your opinion about my worth as a gentleman, I do know my duty to the both of you."

"That does not mean you do not fear it," she replied with conviction. "I think you fear that she is one more person who will turn your life upside down again."

She would. Maids, social schedules, redecorating... he could just envision the mess that would follow. Still—"One cannot overturn a board game when the pieces are already in disarray."

The way Grace stared at him pierced him to his soul. She knew. Somehow, his clumsy words had given him away. "What has changed in you? Because not so long ago, you wanted to marry the diamond at any cost."

Such a complicated question. He could not put his finger on the moment his opinion had changed... except the longer he stayed in England, the more it felt that he was being herded into a place he did not wish to be.

"You do not understand. When I made my wager, Lady Grace, I was not merely foxed. I was impelled. My arrival in London—my seeking a bride—was part of a command performance. One to be undertaken with speed. When one is deprived of the luxuries of time and choice, expediency is all that remains."

He stopped abruptly, tension hardening his jaw. "Once we found her, the choice was then the queen's. Not mine—and most certainly not even hers. I would still have made that choice, had I been asked. I could not live with myself if I would not. But what I want has always been immaterial in the eyes of others."

Grace's lips parted in surprise, and Roland could no longer bear it. He walked on to the next display without her, wanting to walk away from this dangerous conversation, but she caught

*The Ruby Dagger*

up and stepped in front of him, forcing him to stop. "Not to me," she said, her voice firm, her eyes locked upon his.

She would make some man a fine wife. Someday. Hopefully, she found someone worthy of her fierceness. Sensing a change within himself, he shifted his gaze away, directing his attention towards the next item. "You are the only person who has asked about my comfort with my forthcoming nuptials. Even Thorne would fear to ask, and he has been my closest companion since I was seventeen."

"My mama says I have always been the inappropriate sort."

He rubbed his forehead with his fingertips again. "No—I mean, you are the only one who has cared enough to ask. Everyone else expects this to be thrilling to both parties as a matter of course."

Her mouth made the briefest 'O' of understanding, before her brows slammed down in outrage. "Of course I care. You are —" she stopped abruptly, and Roland wondered if she was amending what she was about to say. "You both are good friends to me."

Friends. The word filled him with both pleasure and... no comfort. How strange. "Yes. Friends. I do suppose that is what we are." He smiled at her so that she would know he meant it, but the result was so fragile that he let it drop. "I hope I can also achieve such a rapport with Lady Charity. One day, perhaps."

"One day, perhaps," Grace echoed, and her returned smile looked just as brittle. "If not friends, surely you will find an understanding between one another. Perhaps after she bears your heir. My mama has always said that a good marriage only requires children to form the kernel of happiness."

"I do not agree with your mama," Roland said. There was such bitterness, the words seemed to surprise him as well. Grace subsided, shocked, and Roland had to say more, lest she believe herself at fault for saying something to upset him. "If that were true," he continued in a softer tone of voice, willing her to understand. "Surely, my mother would have been happy." A thought then crossed his mind, and his face darkened. "But I was not enough."

Grace's eyes suddenly misted with tears at his words, and he stepped away again. This time, she let him go, clearly uncertain whether she should follow.

Like most of the people named in Debrett's, there were things about Roland's lineage that everyone took as fact. Gideon Percy, The Breaker of the North, had had two sons. Thaddius Percy—Roland's father—had been the 'spare.' It was no secret that when the duke's elder son died, Thaddius had stepped in to fill the engagement so that they could keep her dowry. Grace would also know that his mother had died bearing what would have been her second child. But neither Debrett's nor history tended to keep a record of... other costs.

Roland looked back at her from the next display, and she took it as an invitation to rejoin him. "I assume then..." Grace said softly, "there was no understanding between your mother and your father?"

"No," he said with a short grunt of laughter. "These days, I suspect my grandfather pressured Thaddius to marry her, for it is his way. If the rumours are true, they despised one another. I was six before she was with child again. Too young, when she died, to have ever wondered what she thought. What she really wanted in life. I suppose I will never know for sure. If their marriage was steeped in hate, it would explain a great deal about their lives—the way my mother was, and about Thaddius," he added.

Grace was watching her feet, nodding to herself. "I think it explains a great deal about you as well."

He straightened. "What do you mean?"

She looked at him, her eyes melancholy once more. "Now, I

*The Ruby Dagger*

think you are reluctant to want more for yourself. It must be hard to want something when you fear it might be taken away. Or when the wants of everyone else always come before your own. I cannot—I cannot even blame you for fearing it. Even I did this to you when I asked you to help me find Charity."

"That is not at all the same." Roland let out a small breath and tilted his head toward her. "A man has a duty to do right by the world. To protect those without the means to protect themselves."

Hearing these words spill from his lips, suddenly Roland was overcome with a sense of wretchedness. "My mother's life is a constant reminder to me that as terrible in some ways as my life has been, at least my title gives me the means to protect myself. More than many others are granted. When I look at Lady Charity—I see that lack of means in her. You ask me if this is what I want. No, I do not want to marry her, Grace. But... that is mostly because I wish her more happiness than I think she will find with me. You love your friend, and after the hardships she has endured, she deserves to find it. I do not think I could offer her love. I offer her the protection of my name, and I worry that it is not enough."

Grace's expression softened, her kind hazel eyes taking no umbrage to his bold words. He could not explain what had possessed him to be so honest with her, to say things he would admit to no one else. But the answer was there, in her forgiving face, free of all judgement.

She lifted her hand, but stopped short of touching him. "As much as it pains me to say, that is the most people such as we can aspire to achieve. Space and freedom to be ourselves. Love-matches are more rare than butterflies in the depths of winter. More fragile, as well. You are a good man, Roland, and you are not your father. You have no need to defend your name to me. With luck, I pray that one day, I, too, will find a man willing to grant me what you offer to Charity." She glanced away, blinking her eyes to keep the tears at bay. "I should go. My father will be expecting me."

Roland let her walk away, for he had no other choice but to do so. The air at his side felt cooler. His arm, upon which hers had rested, was now as cold as ice.

# 20

The next day, Grace was dreading another afternoon lost to paying calls. How could she be expected to prattle on about inanities while a murderer was still on the loose? Yet, she had no excuse to offer her mother, nor anyone to seek out for information. She and Roland were well and truly stuck when it came to making progress on their investigation.

Lady Tilbury's announcement that they were due at the modiste that afternoon arrived like a godsend. At the modiste, Grace's responsibilities were simple. She was to stand still while being fitted. She was not to voice her thoughts on fashion, nor to countermand her mother's choices of fabric and accessories. For once, she had full permission to allow her mind to wander.

There was a second benefit to making a visit to that particular shop. It was an excellent place to catch up on the latest society news. Sooner or later, every woman in high society passed through Madame Moreau's doors. Grace had reason to hope she might uncover some new tidbit or insight, if only she could stumble across the right question.

However, Lady Tilbury had not planned their outing in isolation. When Grace and her mother arrived at Madame

Moreau's, they found Lady Cresswell and Charity awaiting them inside.

Madame Moreau swept over to take charge of her customers. Much like herself, her shop was a blend of French flair and English practicality. Bolts of silk, velvet, and fine lace were artfully displayed, tempting the most discerning of customers. Intricate hats and bonnets, adorned with ribbons, feathers, and even fresh flowers, sat atop pedestals, turning the shop into a veritable garden of fabric wonders.

"Lady Cresswell and Lady Tilbury, it is always a pleasure to have you here. I have just received a new shipment of lace and ribbon, which I set aside for the two of you to see first." Madame Moreau ushered the mothers toward the sitting area in the next room and called for a shopgirl to bring tea.

With the two mamas occupied, Madame Moreau instructed the young women to avail themselves of a nearby fitting room. Heavy velvet drapes separated one fitting room from another, providing a sense of privacy for her customers. Inside, a wooden rack held gowns in various states of production, ready for Grace and Charity to try on.

"Take your time, mesdemoiselles," the modiste said with a wink. "I will keep your mamas busy with my newest arrivals."

Grace and Charity happily accepted the opportunity to chat freely between themselves. They stuck to safe topics such as upcoming balls and suitors while the seamstresses stuck pins in the waists, sleeves, and hems of their new summer walking dresses. When the workers finished their tasks, the young women brushed aside their offers of assistance with changing back into their clothing.

"We can help one another, can we not?" Charity asked Grace.

The seamstresses bobbed curtseys, gathered their pins and scissors, and left the pair on their own.

*The Ruby Dagger*

Finally alone, Grace and Charity moved on to more interesting topics.

"Papa said he saw you at the Sotheby's auction yesterday," Charity said, meeting Grace's gaze in the mirror. "Pray tell, what were you doing there? Were you helping your father with the acquisition of another of his purchases?"

"In part, yes," Grace replied. She lowered her voice before adding, "It gave me an excuse to go along. In truth, Lord Percy suggested I come so that we might question Lord Vaughan."

"And did you? There? In such a public space?"

"Yes, we did," Grace answered. She turned her back so that Charity could do up her buttons. "You would be amazed at how easy it is to have a private conversation in the middle of a crowd, particularly at something like an auction. Everyone else was focused on determining their bids, and had little interest in eavesdropping on anything unrelated."

Charity finished the last button and tied the ribbon at the waist. "So? Did you learn anything? I must say, Lord Vaughan is atop my list of suspicious characters."

Grace motioned for Charity to turn around. "He was my top suspect as well, our only suspect, if I am being honest. Unfortunately, he had a reasonable reply to all of our questions. The man does not have the stolen dagger. I am certain he would covet such a rarity, but he is not the type to stoop to theft and murder to make his acquisitions. He highlighted Prinny's gambling habits and how that was a far easier way to gain access to items owned by the crown."

"Ahh," Charity said with a sigh. "That explains things."

"What things?" Grace drew her brows together in confusion.

"Papa said you and Lord Percy appeared to be in the midst of a rather intense conversation."

Grace's mind drifted back to her talk with Roland. They

had certainly strayed far from their intended purpose. Grace found she had no regrets about that, though. It had eased her heart to learn why Roland remained committed to Charity. Although the result did not change, and Roland and Charity would wed, leaving him far from her reach, at least she now understood he did not do so out of love. Or even out of affection. At least, not out of affection for Charity.

He had said he would not hurt Charity, because Charity was important to Grace. Somehow, that small phrase had meant the world to Grace. It gave her hope that they would find a way to remain friends, at least. Assuming, that is, that her heart could bear being in such close quarters to him once he was lost forever.

Charity cleared her throat, bringing Grace back to the present. "I thought you might have discussed our situation. Mine and Roland's, that is. Perhaps he said something about me?"

Grace froze, her fingers still on the buttons of Charity's dress. Her lack of movement betrayed her as much as any words would have done.

"He did say something. Did you ask, or did he bring it up on his own?" Charity shifted until she could meet Grace's eyes over her shoulder.

Grace's throat closed so tight, not a word dared to go past. Charity's blue eyes grew wide as the silence stretched. Grace swallowed and forced a reply out, surprising herself with her even tone. "No, no. We spoke only of the investigation."

Charity pulled free of Grace's hold on her gown and turned. She grasped onto Grace's arms. "You dropped your gaze, Grace. Why? What are you not telling me?"

Everything, and yet, also nothing. For what could Grace tell her dearest friend? She would no more violate Roland's trust in her than she would tell him of Charity's deepest fears.

*The Ruby Dagger*

"What is it, Grace?" Charity searched her friend's face. "Is it? Does he... Does he want to end the engagement?"

"What? No!" Grace shook free of Charity's hold.

"Then what did he say? Do not fear it will upset me, Grace. I am stronger than I look."

Grace did not need any reminders of Charity's strength. Her friend had survived being kidnapped, had kept her head together enough to plot an escape, and had somehow manoeuvred the queen herself into coming to her aid. Charity was strong enough to survive anything life threw at her.

But Grace was no longer sure she was the same. She could not bear to be caught between Charity and Roland, living with the knowledge that they did not love one another, and were only proceeding with their relationship out of deference to the weighty opinion of the ton. It mattered not that no one else in society would bat an eyelid at such a foundation for a marriage.

The moment Roland and Charity exchanged their vows, Roland would be out of her reach. Grace needed every ounce of courage and strength of spirit to withstand bearing witness to that scene.

That left none for now. None to shore her up so that she might act as a go-between for the pair. Roland would never ask it of her. Charity did not realise the true depths of Grace's growing feelings for Roland. Grace had done too good a job of keeping that secret.

Yet again, she must bite her tongue and let none of her despondency show. She would, however, draw a line.

"Charity, I cannot tell you of my conversations with Lord Percy. You two must learn to speak with one another if you are to make your marriage a success."

Charity's delicate brow wrinkled. "I do not understand. If he said something to you, why would you keep it from me? Am I not your dearest friend?"

"Of course you are!" Grace rushed to reassure her. "But... well, I suppose Lord Percy and I are friends as well. Of a sort. He has so little acquaintances here. And as for me, those who are willing to overlook my predilections for straying outside the lines of society are few and far between."

"So, he has spoken with you. About more than your investigation?"

Grace waved a hand to brush Charity's suggestion aside. "It is nothing, Charity. I am certain that once you two grow more comfortable around one another, he will confide in you. He will have no further need for me then. Admit it. He is hardly the first man to be tongue-tied in your presence." She beamed a wide smile at Charity and prayed it was convincing.

Charity stepped back, putting distance between them. She grabbed her wrap, hat, and gloves from the table. "I should go. Mama and I are due to pay calls this afternoon."

Grace outstretched her hand. "Wait, your buttons. I was not done."

"The shopgirl can do them up." Charity turned to leave, but spun back at the last second. She stared at Grace, as though waiting for her to say something. But Grace had nothing left to add. The silence hung in the air, making a wall between the two friends.

Charity turned on her heel and slipped through the opening in the curtain, leaving Grace behind. Grace dropped into the nearest chair, as always, unconcerned about wrinkles or posture. She pulled at the neck of her dress, fighting against the tightness of her neck and throat.

Her mother found her that way a few minutes later. She stuck her head around the curtain and frowned at her daughter. "Grace! My word! Look at the state of you!"

Grace leapt to her feet and rushed over. "Sorry, Mama. I was lost in thought–"

*The Ruby Dagger*

"I should say so! Where are your gloves and hat? What have you done with your wrap? And your boots? Did you take them off?" Lady Tilbury shooed Grace deeper into the fitting room. "Elsie is waiting by the carriage. I will send her in to set you to rights."

Her mother disappeared with a swish of her skirts. Grace wiped her brow and was amazed to find it dry. It was so hot and cloying and everything felt too tight and itchy against her skin. She moved deeper into the room, hoping to find a draft of air coming from the curtain on the far side. She stopped short when she heard a familiar voice drift from the next room over.

"Madame Moreau, are you certain all is here?" a woman asked.

"Yes, my lady. I checked the packages myself," the modiste replied in her heavily accented English.

Grace laid one finger on the edge of the curtain and twitched it the bare minimum to peek through. Just as she had thought. Lady Fitzroy stood with her back to Grace, her bright blonde hair as recognisable as her voice.

The dowager set her hands on her hips. "We must leave posthaste if we are to make our sailing time. Lark is waiting in the carriage."

"I understand, my lady. That is why I personally reviewed every item before we packed them in the trunks you sent over. There are new wardrobes for you both, just as you ordered."

Lady Fitzroy lifted her chin. "Very well. Call for my footmen. Tell them they may load the trunks onto the carriage."

Madame Moreau left to do Lady Fitzroy's bidding. Grace could not guess why the dowager had remained behind. But then Lady Fitzroy hurried over to the curtain that led to the front of the shop. The one on the opposite side from where Grace stood. Lady Fitzroy checked that no one else was around and then hurried over to the stack of trunks. She opened the first one and then stepped back to reach for something in her pocket.

Her hand pulled free a golden dagger studded with shimmering rubies and diamonds. A priceless dagger that belonged to the Prince Regent of England.

Grace clenched her hands into tight fists and brought one to her mouth to keep herself from saying a word. Through wide eyes, she watched Lady Fitzroy slide the dagger between two dresses and then close the trunk again.

Lady Fitzroy had the stolen dagger, and from what she had said, was due to depart England's shores that very night. There Grace stood, in her stockings, in a fitting room of the modiste. There was no help in sight, not even Charity.

## 21

"It is strange. I have never seen you give up before," Thorne told him.

"That is not exactly fair. We have been turning ourselves in circles all morning, trying to think of an avenue that has gone unexplored. Everything we touch upon breaks apart like ash." Roland's expression was grim as he held his cup, the contents cooling, untouched. "So I am forced to confront the possibility that this battle is lost. Whoever it is, the thief and murderer has well and truly eluded us."

"You cannot lose hope yet. There has to be something we missed." Thorne drummed his fingertips on the table, thinking. And then, abruptly, he stopped, looking struck.

"What is it?" Roland asked him.

It is possible that you said the last part of the puzzle yourself. The thief *and* murderer. We assumed we were looking for one person because the ambassador's gift had been in the same place as the body—but what if there was an accomplice?"

"That could follow." He leaned back, running both hands through his hair in frustration. "On the other hand, that opens up the entire suspect list for suspicion once again."

"Only for now," Thorne assured Roland. "Something at the event was missed. Something we did not know, then, to ask. We must go back to the beginning, to the night of the theft, and ask about what other things the servants witnessed."

"You are suggesting we need to go back to the palace," Roland murmured.

"Aye. If we can, we should seek an appointment to speak with the footmen and butler today. Hopefully, they can make time for us."

"We must to find out, but I must assume the queen, at least, will have motivated them to be responsive to our needs." Calling for Albert, Roland penned a swift note, requesting a convenient time to meet with the butler and some of the footmen, and he sent it off with Wes.

With that, he went upstairs to dress for an appearance at the palace, anticipating a speedy response. Trading his comfortable clothes for breeches and a shirt of fine linen with a high standing collar, he fussed with the choice of his cravat until Thorne finally stepped in to help him.

"Here, let me help you," Thorne said irritably, selecting a silk in light grey. With a few deft moves, Thorne tied it in a simple knot. Neat and appropriate for the day without being flamboyant.

"You do not have to help me with that, truly," Roland told him, meeting Thorne's eyes. "I can tie my cravat."

"It would take you twice as long and you would fuss three times as much," Thorne said dryly. "Besides, you know I do not mind."

"I would hope you would tell me if you did," he said, and Thorne frowned at him.

By the time the frock coat was settled on his shoulders, Wes had come back with a response. The butler would be pleased to

*The Ruby Dagger*

meet with Earl Percy at his convenience, at any point early this afternoon.

"Perfect," Roland said, descending the stairs as they headed to the stable. "Let us see if we cannot find the missing piece, Thorne."

∽

The red brick walls and narrow windows of St James's Palace had been designed less for graciousness and more with thoughts of fortification paramount. It seemed almost as if the old Tudor structure squatted imposingly behind the gatehouse and courtyards, keeping secrets behind its slitted eyes.

But there was nothing secretive or imposing about the staff, who were the very picture of obsequiousness. Within just a few short minutes of his arrival and placement within a private room, the butler hurried to join them.

"Thank you for meeting with me so promptly," Roland began. "I understand you are aware of the nature of my call."

"Of course, Earl Percy," the butler said, inclining his head. "Have you further questions for myself and some of the staff regarding the night the guard was killed in the throne room?"

"Yes," Roland said, wondering how exactly to begin. There had to be something to tease loose. "I need to speak with any of the footmen who were nearby the refreshment rooms, the throne room, and the dining area."

Nodding, the butler at once set things in motion. Within a quarter of an hour, five footmen joined them in the room. Though Thorne stood casually behind him, the skin between his shoulders itched. Like him, Thorne was at high attention, studying the men for any sign of nervousness.

Among the five, one of them was the footman who Roland had sent to get the queen. He was the footman assigned to stand by the privacy rooms, just around the corner from where the guard was killed.

As good a place to start as any, he resolved, turning to the man. "Are you absolutely certain that the guests who used the privacy rooms did not avail themselves of any servants' corridors attached?"

"I do not believe so, my lord. Sir Julian—he was the only one who could have," the man said briefly, and Roland nodded for him to continue. He and Thorne had known about that exit from the beginning. "Sir Julian was... well occupied by the sounds of things."

Likely dealing with dyspepsia, and in a fashion the servant overheard. Warming to the subject, Roland moved onto the next possibility. "What about the women's rooms?" Roland asked him, for he recalled they had been down the hall and on the other side of the corridor from the men's rooms.

But the footman shook his head. "The women's rooms have no servant access, and as I told Sir David, only Lady Fitzroy and Lady Grace Tilbury used them during that time."

"Yes, I recall you told him also that Lady Fitzroy dropped her fan," Roland said, grasping at straws. "Did Lady Fitzroy meet with anyone else while she was about?"

"She exchanged words with Lady Grace for just a moment on her way to use the privacy room."

"On her way *to* the room. You are certain?" The man agreed, and Roland frowned. "How much time passed between that and when I bid you to find the queen?"

"Perhaps ten minutes, Lord Percy?" the man considered, his brow furrowing in thought. "Mayhap closer to a quarter hour."

If Grace left the room before Lady Fitzroy, then Lady Fitzroy would not have been able to commit the murder. The deed had already been done by then. But it was not out of the

*The Ruby Dagger*

realm of possibility she may have served as some other sort of distraction.

"And Lady Fitzroy returned to the dinner before I sought you," Roland confirmed. "Tell me about her fan. She dropped it in front of you?"

"No, my lord. It must have fallen from her wrist while she was leaving the women's room, and she noticed it missing just before she turned the corner to go back to the dining room. She called for my attention and asked me to go retrieve it for her."

Thorne cleared his throat softly. The sound was barely audible, but Roland picked up on his interest. She had asked the footman to take an action that would turn him away from watching her. At the corner of the hall, there was a large potted plant. It was conceivable someone might use it as a point to drop something small for someone else to pick up. But on the other hand, perhaps it was a coincidence.

Still, if he figured the time of it correctly, Lady Fitzroy had lost her fan, sent the footman to retrieve it, and returned to dinner just as Grace and Roland had been inside of the throne room, discovering the body.

Something about her timing was suspicious, and Roland couldn't quite discern the shape of it. If she had been a few moments later, or had Roland left the throne room sooner, they would have seen one another.

"Let us talk about what happened earlier than Lady Grace and Lady Fitzroy's visits. From where you were posted, you could observe each gentleman as they approached from around the corner near where the throne room was. Is that right? And you would know if they did not return that direction?"

The footman hesitated briefly. "Mostly, that is correct. But... Sir David Green did not come from the direction of the throne room and dining hall, as the others did, when he came to where I was stationed."

Roland frowned. "Did you find that curious?"

"No, Lord Percy. If you travel the length of this hall, it circles a good portion of the main level of the palace. Sir David would be familiar with that fact. All it meant was that he had taken the hallway in the other direction while attending to his business."

Satisfied, Roland let it go. "Did anyone else pass your direction in the hallway during the dinner portion? Other servants, perhaps?"

"Just Bailey, here, your lordship, as he came from the offices for the head of the guards. They are some distance down the hall from the refreshment rooms."

Roland turned his head to the footman named Bailey, who stood with his hands clasped politely behind his back. "You were not, then, stationed near the dinner itself?"

"Yes, my lord, I was sent to request Sir David's presence at his earliest convenience, but I did not linger in the halls, and I do not know if I can assist much. I passed along my message and came back straightaway."

"Did you escort him to his destination?"

"No, my lord. He was in the middle of dinner and told me that he would be along shortly."

Sir David had been called away by a footman early in the dinner—Roland recalled Thorne mentioning it. "You noticed nothing untoward in the hallways?" The man shook his head in negation. "Do you remember if the guard was still on duty outside of the throne room?"

"Yes, my lord. He was there and standing at attention both times I passed him," Bailey confirmed.

"Do you remember when exactly you went to find Sir David?"

"I am sorry, I cannot be quite exact... but it was sometime

*The Ruby Dagger*

after the main course had been served. The plates were still on the table."

At least they knew that the guard could not have been dead before then. Roland wondered if Sir David had noted whether the guard was there at the time of his passing. He must have, he reasoned, for surely the man would have noted or mentioned it.

"Who was looking for Sir David?" Roland asked next. "Who dispatched you?"

"The captain of the guard, Lord Percy," the footman said. "I was posted near the office."

"I do not suppose you know why the captain was looking for Sir David?" he asked next, but the man shook his head.

"I am sorry. All I know is that someone had arrived at the guardhouse asking for him."

Glancing behind himself, Roland noted Thorne's slightly narrowed eyes. He had the uneasiest sense that he had finally stumbled across the loose thread in the tapestry of the mystery, and he did not like where it was pointing. Hopefully, there was more.

He turned back to the butler and the footmen. "Thank you for your help. Is it possible I could request the time of the captain? I have a few questions I must ask him."

The butler bobbed his greying head, dismissing the footmen back to their duties. "Of course, Lord Percy. I will send for him at once."

## 22

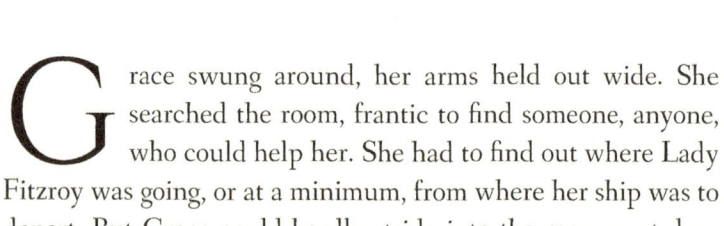

Grace swung around, her arms held out wide. She searched the room, frantic to find someone, anyone, who could help her. She had to find out where Lady Fitzroy was going, or at a minimum, from where her ship was to depart. But Grace could hardly stride into the room next door and make demands. Lady Fitzroy would be more likely to strike her down than answer questions, particularly given she had a stolen priceless dagger in her trunk.

Grace had to get Roland. He would come up with a way to stop her. He had connections to the military. If that did not work, they could go together to the queen and tell her all.

Grace's roaming gaze landed on her kid-skin boots. She dropped into a chair and pulled them onto her feet. She was nearly done tying the laces when Elsie came in to assist her. She motioned for Elsie to come close.

"I must go to Roland. Lady Fitzroy has the dagger and is planning to flee the country," Grace whispered.

A string of emotions flitted across Elsie's features—shock, confusion, horror. But she did not ask how Grace had learned this information, nor if there was a chance Grace was mistaken.

*The Ruby Dagger*

Her features settled into a display of obedience. "What do you need me to do?"

"Her trunks are being loaded onto the carriage now. See if you can find out where they are going. But be subtle," Grace added. "Do not put yourself at risk."

"What of you? Your mama? How will you explain it to her?"

Grace's mouth tightened. Her mother would ask far too many questions, slowing Grace down exactly when she had to make haste. Her mother would be absolutely livid, but there was no choice for it. Grace had to go on her own.

"I will slip out the back and flag a hansom to take me to Roland's home. Tell my mother I was gone when you got here. If you can find out where Lady Fitzroy is headed, offer to go look for me so you can bring the information to us. I will tell Thorne to remain behind to await you."

Elsie wrung her hands, but again, she did not argue. When Grace made to leave, Elsie reached out to stop her. "You will need money for the hack, miss." She rifled through her pocket and produced a few coins.

Grace took her offer, never so grateful for the loyalty of her lady's maid. "I will repay you in full. I promise." With that, she dropped the coins into her pocket, grabbed her gloves and hat, and dashed out the back of the shop.

The shop opened onto a narrow alley cast in perpetual shade by the tall buildings on either side. Grace hiked up her skirt and scooted around the piles of rubbish that had piled up behind the shops and cafes, but did not bother to watch for puddles. Ruining her shoes was the least of her worries.

Fortune smiled at her. A cab pulled over just as she reached the end of the alleyway. She waited until the passenger descended and moved away before calling out to the driver. "Grosvenor Square, as fast as you can," she ordered before providing Roland's full address.

The driver cast her a narrow-eyed gaze, curious about a young maiden going there on her own. Grace pulled a coin from her pocket and tossed it up to him. Money was enough to convince him to hold his tongue.

Still, his reaction served as a warning for Grace. She pulled the curtains shut to hide her face from passing eyes. She jolted and rattled with every rumble of the carriage wheels. The cheap, torn seating offered no cushion at all. Grace gritted her teeth and focused her mind on her task. Get to Roland. Tell him what she saw. Go with him to stop Lady Fitzroy.

The carriage stopped in front of Roland's front door. Grace tugged her wrap up over her head until it hid her face from view. She did not wait for someone to assist her with her descent. Throwing caution and dignity to the wind, she scrambled down the narrow steps, giving thanks she did not trip over her skirt. She hurried up the front steps to the front door and rapped on the heavy brass knocker.

The thuds echoed inside the townhouse, but no one answered. Grace could not stand on the doorstep, where anyone might see her. Roland would certainly understand. She tried the handle and found it to be unlocked. She slipped inside.

A man appeared at the other end of the corridor, his bright white hair like a ghost in the dark hall. He came closer, his serene countenance never changing, despite the strange woman standing in Lord Percy's front vestibule. His suit was impeccably pressed, and his demeanour steady. "Can I help you?"

"I need Roland—Lord Percy, or Mr Thorne?" Grace blurted. "I am Lady–"

"Lady Grace," the man said. "Lord Percy has spoken of you. I am Albert Archer, his lordship's butler."

Grace's heart beat slowed enough for her to catch her

*The Ruby Dagger*

breath. "Oh, thank goodness! Is he here? Can you show me to him?"

"I am terribly sorry, but he and Mr Thorne have gone out."

Grace was undeterred. "When will they be back? Where have they gone?"

"I am not sure. They requested a meeting with the butler at St James's. They did not tell me when to expect them back."

More questions rose unbidden in Grace's mind. How long ago had Roland left? Where else might he be? Should she go to the palace and try to find him there?

Valid though they were, they were questions that would not help her right now. She had to stop Lady Fitzroy, and every moment of delay heightened the chances that she would leave England before they caught her. Grace needed proof of the dowager's guilt. All along, she had been certain Lady Fitzroy was somehow involved, yet no one had believed her. If she burst into the palace on her own, making wild claims, the queen might not listen. And then what?

Grace was loath to admit it, but she required the support of someone else if she was to convince the queen to act. Roland would believe her, of that she was sure. But with him unavailable, she had no idea where to turn next.

"My lady," Albert said in a gentle tone. "Please, allow me to assist you, if I may. His lordship would not want you to be running about London on your own." He indicated the nearest doorway and waited for Grace to go inside.

Grace found herself in a drawing room. Much like the dining room she had seen on her last visit, this, too, was only half furnished. Now, however, the decor was the least of her concerns. She walked to the nearest chair and perched on the edge of the seat, prepared to move as soon as she decided which way to go.

The butler followed her into the room and went to stand

where she could see his face, but far enough away as to not loom over her. He clasped his hands behind his back and stood, ready to take her orders.

But where to begin? What did the butler know about their current task? He must be aware of some of it, for he recognised her easily enough and asked no questions as to why she burst into Roland's home. Grace decided to skip straight to the crux of the matter.

"Lady Fitzroy is preparing to flee the country. She has in her possession the Prince Regent's stolen dagger. I saw her with it—this is not supposition on my part. I need Roland's help to stop her before she can get away."

The butler did not blink an eye at her statement. "Yes, I can see the need for urgency. I will send the children to look for Lord Percy."

"Thank you," Grace said, and she meant it. Though the man was simply doing his job, she was grateful he did not question the veracity of her statements. He took them as fact and acted accordingly.

"Would you care to wait here, my lady?"

Grace's stomach lurched at the thought of sitting idle. She shifted in her chair, nervous energy preventing her from waiting comfortably. There were far too many what-ifs in play, but the largest was the uncertainty about how quickly the children might locate Roland. She pressed a hand to her forehead and demanded her mind settle long enough to allow logic to take over.

The list of people aware of the situation was short—Roland and Thorne, who were otherwise occupied, Charity, who was of no help now, Queen Charlotte, who might not listen. Grace required power and importance, someone who would not presume that Grace's previous experiences with Lady Fitzroy were colouring her thoughts now.

*The Ruby Dagger*

One name floated to the surface. Sir David Green. Roland had shown a high level of trust in the man. The former military commander certainly had the gravitas to send soldiers chasing after the Fitzroy carriage.

"Sir David Green—do you happen to have his address?" she asked.

"A wise choice, my lady. And yes, I do. If you will wait a moment, I will have the children harness the horses to the carriage and I will ferry you there myself."

"Thank you, but that will take too long. If you can help me flag a hansom cab and give the driver the address, I will be on my way. The Sprouts can set off to find Lord Percy that much sooner."

"Of course. I will make sure Wes passes along the message of where you are bound and what you have learned."

It took only a few minutes to convey the importance of their assignment to the boy. Wes stood tall before her, eager to do his part. If he had any fear of racing through London on his own, he did not show it. Likely as not, he felt none. The children had, after all, survived on the streets for a time.

Before climbing into the cab, Grace asked the butler to keep an eye out for Elsie. She used the carriage ride to put her thoughts into order. Unlike with Roland, she would have to offer a modicum of explanation. In point of fact, she was not sure that Sir David Green was even aware of her involvement. She refused to consider that he might not be at home either. Fortune was said to favour the bold. Today, that was Grace.

The carriage driver brought Grace to a part of London she had not visited before. The houses were less grand than the ones near her own, but the flowers blooming in the window boxes proclaimed a certain pride of ownership. Grace's worries that she might be recognised eased. These were not the homes of families who could afford the cost of a London season, no matter how upright they were.

A butler answered the door and his eyes grew wide to find a young lady alone on the doorstep.

"Might I speak with Sir David Green?" Grace asked, in her haughtiest tone. "It is with regard to an urgent matter."

The butler ushered her inside and hurried off to check with his master. He returned a minute later and led her to Sir David's study without delay. She recognised Sir David Green, having seen him on the night of the state dinner, even though she had not spoken with him.

Roland's former commander sat behind a vast mahogany desk that dominated his dimly lit study. His hair, streaked with grey early from his military campaigns, was neatly combed back. His posture was impeccably straight, likely a residual marker of his military bearing, and he wore a dark blue coat, not unlike those of his former regiment, with subtle, polished brass buttons.

Oak bookshelves lined the walls, but it was the large, detailed map of the Iberian Peninsula, dotted with annotations and battle sites from the Peninsular War, that captured Grace's attention. Nearby, a glass-encased shelf displayed various military decorations, and a prominently featured, well-polished sabre with an intricately designed hilt.

Though they had not been introduced, his eyes lit with a hint of recognition, though he did not seem able to place her. The solemn expression on her face was enough for him to decide to dismiss the butler and offer her a chair.

"Sir David, my name is Lady Grace Tilbury. I have been assisting Lord Percy with the matter of the stolen dagger." Grace took a deep breath and ploughed onward. "I know the identity of the thief and murderer. I need your help to see them caught and brought to justice."

# 23

The captain of the guard was in his late thirties, exuding an air of the breeding of nobility, but tempered by the stern demeanour of a man of service. It had taken nearly twenty minutes for him to appear when summoned, leaving Roland to try not to fidget while they waited in the empty room.

"I apologise for my delay, Lord Percy," the man said, just a trace of his Irish brogue colouring his words. He stood at parade rest after according Roland a slight bow. "I was patrolling the grounds when the footman sought me out."

"You do not have to apologise to me for doing your duty," Roland said with a nod, and the captain inclined his head graciously. "I only wanted to discuss with you some of the events that happened the night of the ambassador's state dinner. Please, Captain O'Neil, take a seat."

The captain straightened his coat and settled himself in the indicated chair. "Of course. I am at your service, my lord."

The captain did not look uncomfortable or dismayed by Roland's presence, but there was a heaviness about him that had not been there a moment ago. He carried the burden for the guard who had fallen on his watch, and Roland respected him for that. "Allow me to express my deepest condolences, as well, for the loss of your man, Captain."

"Your words are appreciated, Lord Percy," the man replied, his shoulders lifting slightly. "Sergeant Richardson was a good man and soldier. It grieves us all for him to be felled in such a manner."

Roland thought about the best way to begin, and in the end, decided for straightforwardness. He did not truly believe the captain of the guard could be a suspect. "Did anything untoward happen that evening before you were notified of Sergeant Richardson's murder in the throne room?"

To his credit, the captain considered this inquiry seriously, his brows drawing together as he reviewed the night. "No, Lord Percy. Not to my knowledge. None of the other guards encountered any difficulties or strange visitors. I saw nothing unusual on the rounds I made, and the evening was otherwise a quiet one."

"I understand, however, that you sent a footman by the name of Bailey to find Sir David Green at the dinner."

"Yes, that is correct."

Studying the captain, Roland noted that O'Neil did not look concerned in any way. "Why did you send for him?"

"Mr Green showed up during the course of the event." O'Neil made fists of his hands—the only sign of his discomfort in relating the details of the story. "The lad seemed distressed, and he begged entry to see his father."

"Curious. Did he say why?"

"Not directly, my lord. He said only that he had got news, and that it was urgent. Mr Green mentioned that Sir David gave him directions to come to the Palace and inform him straight away if that news arrived during the evening."

Frowning, Roland considered this. "I assume you let him in?"

"Of course," Captain O'Neil said, sitting upright.

"And then what happened?" Roland prompted him.

"I sent him to wait in a private room near the offices and then sent Bailey to notify Sir David to meet with me for the sake of discretion."

Puzzle pieces began to fall together within Roland's head, and he made an effort to control the expression on his face. "Thank you for your assistance, Captain. Do you know at approximately what time Mr Green departed?"

O'Neil did not consider for long. "It was just after eleven, for I remember the ringing of the bells."

Roland stood up. "I do not wish to keep you from your duties for an unduly long period of time. Have a good afternoon, Captain."

"And to you as well, Lord Percy. I wish you luck in finding the man responsible for our loss."

To that, Roland could not formulate much of a reply, because he was afraid he had found the man after all. He sat back down again in the empty room, thinking very hard. Surely he must be miscalculating things.

He sat for so long, Thorne entered the room to see what was the matter. "Lord Percy?" he said, adopting the formal voice that he addressed Roland with in public. "Is something the matter?"

"Mr Green was on site the night of the murder," Roland began slowly. "His arrival was what prompted the captain of the guard to send for Sir David sometime before eleven."

Comprehension filtered slowly across Thorne's solemn face, leeching some of his colour with it. "You believe that one of the two men is the murderer—either Sir David or his son."

"I do not believe the water is even that muddy. Of the two

men, who do you truly think would have wielded the hunting knife?"

"Sir David Green," Thorne said with a small sigh, dropping his voice low. "The one with the military background, who would be most familiar with using a knife to kill." He paused, considering the matter further. He then added, "The one whom the guard would not fight, not expecting the attack."

Roland's face pinched with anguish. "Yes. That is the conclusion I have also come to. How culpable his son is, I cannot be sure, but at the least, I believe that at the very least, David instructed Matthew to come to the palace and serve as an excuse for him to leave the table."

"But... why, Roland?" While he had fewer interactions than Roland had with Sir David, Thorne had trusted and respected his superior, considering him quite able. This was a blow to the man in his estimation, as well. "Why would he steal from the crown and murder a guard? It does not make any sense."

"I cannot imagine," Roland replied at first, feeling a numbness set in through his extremities. "Unless... perhaps he was desperate somehow." Another piece of the puzzle fell into place. "Thorne, do you remember how Fitzroy pointed me towards Matthew as a person who might know who was attending the gambling hells?"

Thorne nodded. "Yes. You suspect that Matthew may have had an issue with gambling."

"It would follow. At the Horse Guard Parade, David mentioned to me he had come back to London to deal with financial matters. And he was nearly apoplectic to discover that his son had been at the Scarlet Jack the night of the fire. I thought it was anger about the risk to his person—but what if it was because he had only recently resolved the issue of Matthew's debts?"

Thorne nodded, pinching the bridge of his nose. "The fire

*The Ruby Dagger*

started at the back office of The Scarlet Jack. Fire would be a convenient method to dispose of a record of debt." His eyes flickered beneath his lids. "And he has the murder weapon in his possession. He banked upon our taking his word for it that there was no maker's mark. No means of incriminating him as the owner of it."

Roland covered his face with his hands, breathing through the pain of being played the fool. Sir David had been like a father to him after he had departed from Northumberland. That he was complicit in such a terrible crime ate at his soul. "We may castigate ourselves until the stars fall," he said, resolving to set things to rights. "But there are actions we must hurry to take. We have tipped our hand in speaking with the captain of the guard and word of our visit will find its way back to him, eventually. It is only a matter of time before he ties up whatever remaining loose ends are there to find."

"Where would you like me to begin?" Thorne asked him.

"I want you to track down the proprietor of The Scarlet Jack. The hard evidence may be gone, but for now, the circumstantial remains. See if the man recalls Matthew Green. I would be surprised if the owner of a gambling hell would not recall who stood among its debtors. Find out also if he knows whether those debts have been paid—and by whom. We are likely to find a link, and I wish to find it before the proprietor of The Scarlet Jack encounters an unfortunate accident."

"At once," Thorne told him.

With the needful said, the two men made their way out of the palace and back to their horses. Astride, Roland pressed his heels to Arion's sides to signal a fast trot, and Horse—Thorne's mount—threw his head up as he joined in the spirit of a good exercise.

"Find me back at the house the moment you have word," he told his man, and with cautious speed, he made his way back home. To pace. To wait. To write an urgent letter to Grace, informing her of the news.

But as he rode up the streets in the direction of Grosvenor and his townhouse, he spied a familiar sprite pelting on foot in the opposite direction, back towards the palace. Wheeling Arion about, he hailed the boy. "Wes!"

"Lord Percy!" the boy slowed to a halt, only slightly winded. "I was coming to find you."

"And you found me," Roland said with a small smile so that he wouldn't intimidate the lad. "What is the matter?"

"Lady Grace—she stopped by the house. She said..." his brows screwed up as he tried to remember her exact words. "'Lady Fitzroy had the dagger.'"

Lady Fitzroy had the ambassador's dagger? Roland stiffened as he tried to put this new information into the context of his thoughts, and Arion danced beneath him at the change in his posture. The boy reached up to hold the horse's head, stroking the nose to soothe him.

"Is Grace still waiting at the house?" he asked Wes. It must be the debts, he reasoned. Perhaps Matthew's debts were how Lady Fitzroy had bent David to her will.

The boy shook his head in negation. "When she found out that neither you nor Mr Thorne were at home, she told Albert that she could not wait. Lady Fitzroy was preparing to depart the city, and she needed to find help to stop her."

Sudden terror wormed in his guts, and though he was not a deeply religious sort, he found himself uttering a silent prayer. "Wes, where did she go? Where was Lady Grace going to seek help?"

The boy looked askance at him, seeing Roland's alarm. "She said she was going to Sir David Green for help to rouse the guard to help intercept her, Lord Percy."

With the war on in France, Lady Fitzroy was unlikely to

*The Ruby Dagger*

make for France. Roland cursed himself, thinking of Peregrine's 'chance' meeting with the ambassador. She had her sights set on Europe. She would head east, to Hamburg or Lubeck, perhaps even Sweden. The nearest port for ships going that way was Gravesend.

His heart stuttered in his chest, and Roland could barely gasp out instructions to the boy "Go back home!" he ordered the boy. "Alert Albert and send him to find the Captain of the Guard at the palace. Tell him to mobilise the guard. They must make haste to intercept the Fitzroy family. They are likely on route to Gravesend, but he should not exclude other possibilities. Go now!"

Wes took off at a sprint even as Roland seized the reins and kicked Arion into a full gallop, tearing off in the direction of Hyde Park.

Duty would require him to head off in pursuit of the Fitzroys. Queen Charlotte and Prinny had been most adamant about the necessity of retrieving the stolen dagger. It was not just a gift. It was the symbol of a newly forged connection between two countries.

If he did not set off straight away, Lady Fitzroy would gain a lead on any pursuers that most likely would secure her escape. He doubted Albert would be able to rouse a fast enough response from the palace to catch her.

Yet, that knowledge was not enough to cause him to deviate from his current route. He had told Grace that Sir David was trustworthy. He was the reason she had gone to the man's home. It was his fault that she had walked into the den of a man who had killed and committed arson to cover his trail.

Part of him still refused to accept that Sir David was capable of such violence. It was hard to reconcile the man he had served underneath with one who could raise a hand against an innocent woman. But the man guilty of these crimes was not the man he knew.

Roland leaned forward and clicked his heels against Arion's flank again. He whispered desperate words, urging the horse to give its all to the chase. The heavy racket of the hooves on the cobblestones were enough to warn passersby to get out of the way. Roland's vision narrowed until all he saw was the road before him.

Lady Fitzroy and the dagger be damned. He would face whatever consequences the queen handed out for his failure to apprehend the Fitzroys. He could not force his thoughts to follow duty to the queen.

His heart had already chosen its duty to Grace instead.

## 24

"You know who the killer is?" Sir David Green said from his seat behind his desk. He leaned forward and rested his hands on the desk. "Who? How? The last time I spoke with Roland, he did not indicate he had made such progress. How can you have suddenly found the culprit?"

Grace fought the urge to leap to her feet and demand he get moving. Sir David was old enough to be her father, not a young buck ready to ride to the rescue. "I have my methods, Sir David."

Sir David continued speaking. "Is Lord Vaughan the one behind all this? He was at the state dinner and at the Scarlet Jack the night of the fire. Few in London would covet that dagger more than him."

While his statement was true, he was on the wrong track, just as they had been. Grace needed to take control over the conversation.

"It is not Lord Vaughan."

"Sir Julian, then?"

"No, sir. It was neither of them. If you will kindly cede the floor, I will explain everything. We must hurry if we are to catch her."

"Her?" Sir David sat up straight. "There was no woman involved."

"That is what everyone said, but we were wrong. There was one woman walking around the palace corridors that night. I do not know how she managed to kill the guard, but she most definitely has the ruby dagger. I witnessed her holding it, no more than an hour ago. She said she was on her way to board a ship. If we do not move fast, she will escape capture."

"Who is this woman?" Sir David demanded in a sharp tone.

"Lady Fitzroy," Grace replied. She waited for Sir David to leap into action, but he did no such thing. Instead, the colour leached from his face.

"You are certain she has Prinny's ruby dagger? The one gifted to him by the ambassador?"

"Of course I am!" Grace gasped in frustration. "I was there when the ambassador presented it to the royals. I paused to take in the display before we proceeded to dinner. There can be no mistaking it, sir."

"How did you come to witness her with it? Were you at her home?"

Grace gripped onto her skirt. "We are wasting time, Sir David. If we do not act quickly, she will escape."

"So you say, but this is a far-fetched tale. You must share everything if I am to convince others."

"Fine," Grace said with a nod of her head. "I was at the modiste. Lady Fitzroy came into the fitting room beside mine. She was there to collect a new wardrobe. I overheard her discussion with Madame Moreau, and the madame herself assured her all was ready. The modiste left to call for the footmen to bring the packed trunks to the carriage. While she

*The Ruby Dagger*

was out of the room, Lady Fitzroy pulled the dagger from her pocket, opened one of the trunks, and tucked it between the folded clothes."

"And this was an hour ago, you say?"

"Yes. I got away as quickly as I could and flagged a hackney to bring me to Lord Percy's home. He was not there. I recalled Lord Percy speaking highly of you and the assistance you had offered early on. I decided to come straight here, while Lord Percy's butler sent the stableboy off with a message."

"Did Lady Fitzroy indicate where she was going? Did she mention the name of the port?"

Grace bit her lip. "She did not. I left my lady's maid behind with instructions to ferret out that information. If she can learn anything of value, she will make her way to Lord Percy's to alert us."

Was it her mistake, or had Sir David relaxed at Grace's words? His behaviour had drifted so far beyond the bounds of her imagination that she no longer knew what to make of it. On the way over, she had accepted that it might take some convincing to get him to act. This, however, went beyond a simple explanation.

The military man placed his palms together and lifted them to his face, taking on a position of deep contemplation. Grace fumbled for what else she could say or do to properly convey the urgency of the matter. She glanced around the room, searching for inspiration. All she observed were remnants from his days as the commander of His Majesty's army. She was not familiar enough with his reputation to determine whether he was normally quick to action or someone who considered all the options before making a move. At this moment, she needed the former.

Her gaze landed on the desk that sat between them. Papers

littered the surface, some arranged in rough stacks, others strewn about. A bottle of ink stood in one corner, but the quill to accompany it was not in its place. If she could find the quill, she could get Sir David to scribble a few words on a piece of foolscap. He did not even need to rouse himself. His request and his signature would be enough.

Grace looked again at the man, but he had a far off look in his eyes as he stared into space. What he had to contemplate, she did not know. Was it not a simple matter to say yes?

She shifted in her chair to get a better view of the desk. It was then that she noticed a leather handle sticking out from under a piece of paper. There was something about it that rang familiar. It was not far from her. She had only to reach out and grab it.

Before she could think better of it, she did just that. It slid free without a sound and barely a flutter of the page. Her hand wrapped around the handle. She marvelled at the solid weight of it, despite not being overly large. Dark stains marred the knife's surface. She tilted the knife to better catch the light, and that was when she saw the shiny gold band encircling the butt of the handle.

Grace dropped the knife onto the desk with a clatter, rousing Sir David from his deep thoughts. "I am sorry, sir. I was looking for a quill to send a note to Lord Percy," she blathered.

Sir David glanced down and saw the knife now sitting on top of his desk. His eyes narrowed. "Tell me, Lady Grace, why our queen gave you permission to take part in a murder investigation."

Grace hardly registered his words. Her thoughts were fully occupied by the memory of the last time she had seen that very knife. It had been sticking from the chest of the royal guard. She had noted then, as now, the frayed edge of the leather wrap

*The Ruby Dagger*

where it met the golden butt. Those dark stains were not shadows, but dried blood.

Sir David was meant to have the knife, she reminded herself. He had offered to check it for a maker's mark or some other identifying information that would point them in the direction of its owner. But why, then, was it still stained with blood? Why hadn't he removed the leather wrap? Why was it lying, forgotten, on the desk in his study?

"My lady? I asked you a question."

Grace pulled her gaze from the knife. "I helped Lord Percy before. Lady Charity is my dearest friend. I impressed the queen with my dedication."

"When did you first speak with them regarding this matter?"

Grace's mouth dried. "At the state dinner."

Sir David's gaze slipped down to the knife before he settled it on Grace's face. "I think you were involved because you saw the body."

Grace's head dipped in a nod.

Sir David shot up from his chair. He grabbed the knife from the desk. His fierce expression sent ice sliding down Grace's spine.

Grace slid out of her chair and resisted the urge to stand straight and run for the day. She hunched her shoulders to make herself smaller. "I am sorry to have bothered you, Sir David. I can see you are a busy man. I will return to Lord Percy's to wait for his help."

Sir David circled around the desk. Grace backed closer to the shelves lining the wall, careful to keep the chair between them. She chanced a look at the door. Had it always been so far away?

She would never make it there before he fell upon her. Truly, his expression was murderous.

Everyone had told Grace that Lady Fitzroy was not the killer. Roland had stressed the impossibility that a woman could have felled the guard with a single blow.

But Sir David, a military man with an extensive career, knew exactly where to strike.

There was no denying that truth now, not when he again held the murder weapon in his hand.

## 25

Roland was in such a lather when he arrived that he simply hitched Arion to a nearby post by the front door rather than circle around to the stable. So when David's butler answered, he was not sure whether the man was more surprised by the horse being there, or by Roland's intense appearance.

"Lord Percy?" the butler said, looking most confused. "Can I assist you?"

"Lady Grace," Roland demanded. "Is she here?"

The butler frowned. "Yes, the lady is upstairs with Sir David in his study as we speak."

Had he arrived in time to thwart her misadventure? He prayed that he had. With a quick breath to calm himself, Roland's mind girded itself for the possibility of a coming battle. He raked his gaze over the butler once more, noting that the man did not seem secretive or discomposed. How much was he involved in his master's treachery? All? Or none of it?

Roland elected for guile, and made a quick excuse, keeping his voice low as he entered the house. "I am sorry for my rush, but there is an urgent matter at hand."

"So Lady Grace said. I will escort you upstairs to them," Collins said, preparing to lead him upstairs.

"No. No need to trouble yourself. She has surely told Sir David to expect me. Just point the way, and I will join them."

"Sir David's study can be found on the first floor—turn left, the second door on the right," Collins explained, looking even more confused. "Shall I arrange to have your horse moved to the stables?"

"If you like, but there is no need; my errand, hopefully, will not take long."

Bobbing his head, Collins wandered out of the hallway, and Roland took the steps upstairs two at a time, trying to be as silent as possible. After finding the door to David's study, he flung it open to find a most chilling sight.

The room was long, a desk along the right-hand wall, and bookshelves along the left, but there was nothing serene about the study. Sir David had rounded the desk to approach Grace, putting himself neatly between her and the door, and worse, he was holding a knife. Grace was backed up against the bookshelves, looking terrified.

He could come to only one conclusion. Sir David knew everything, and far too late, Grace had discovered the full truth as well. And here Roland stood, having just visited the palace—utterly unarmed of everything but his wits.

At least his entry had done one thing of purpose. Sir David's advance towards her halted as he turned to face his newest threat. And as he did so, Grace managed to snatch a pewter candlestick from one of the nearby tables, folding it in her skirts.

To whatever credit remained to him, David looked sick at heart to be found here, but resolute. He understood that he would be condemned to the gallows if his resolve should waver. With the truth exposed, he would be deadly dangerous now—a

*The Ruby Dagger*

man with truly nothing to lose in killing either one of them, unless he could be swayed to reason.

"Sir David," Roland beseeched softly, flinging out his hand in appeal. "Lay down your weapon. Please."

The shadows on Sir David's face grew longer. "Why? Why did it have to be you to be involved in this business, lad? It was nearly resolved, and with no further harm needing to be done."

"Because I swore to do my duty to those in need," Roland said, heartbroken. "As you taught me to do."

Sir David's lips lifted in a small smile, full of pride and sorrow. "I did not have to teach you such things. You are a good lad. A better man than your father and grandfather, for certain. Even as a stripling with little more than the other boy in tow with you, I could see you were a protector with a streak of rash nobility from the very start."

Sir David took one step backwards, moving Grace into his line of sight while maintaining his focus on Roland standing by the door. "I do not want to do this," he told Roland. "But if you can bend your principles just this once, perhaps we may find a way out for all of us."

"For all of us!" Grace spluttered, and Roland shot her a glare, insisting she be silent. "You would have us let Lady Fitzroy steal from the crown without consequence? Roland and Thorne said you were a man of honour!"

He seemed to ignore her words, keeping his eyes locked upon Roland, but he answered her in a despondent, gravelly tone. "Young woman, some things supersede matters of the crown. Family is one of those matters. Roland, you understand this."

"Your son's gambling debts made the bridle set upon your head, but who held your lead, Sir David?" Roland said tightly. "Was it truly Lady Fitzroy?" Sir David's head bowed slightly in agreement. "So the fire then had nothing to do with Prinny. You were only disposing of the ledgers. She paid the debt, and you wanted to hide your affiliation."

"I had to," Sir David said, his eyes pleading with Roland. "Matthew's debts nearly ruined us, and only Lady Fitzroy's intervention saved us from scandal. I did not know—I did not imagine—that her assistance came with such strings until I found myself primed as a weapon to be aimed at the crown. Nor did I expect that the man I hired determined of his own volition to use the incident to hide the records of his own debts. No one was supposed to be harmed. Please, tell me you understand."

Roland's very soul felt raw with anguish at this betrayal. "There is a part of me that does understand, but still... I cannot condone it. Lay down the weapon, Sir David. I beg you. I will go on my knees to the queen, seeking clemency for you if I must. All I ask is that you set the knife down now."

The older man sighed in regret. "I believe you truly would. But some things are not so easily forgiven, Roland."

Swiftly—so swiftly that neither of them had a moment to react—Sir David's sideways step put him in arm's reach of Grace. In one fluid motion, he pulled her close, pressing the cold, sharp point of the hunting knife against her throat, where the rapid beat of her pulse thrummed. Grace had only a chance to make the faintest squeak of alarm before freezing completely, her body rigid against his.

Sir David held his breath, his hand unyielding as he waited for Roland to absorb the full horror of the scene unfolding before him. Roland's gaze swept over Grace, where the slightest tremble of her lips and the stoop of her shoulders painted a portrait of acceptance woven with despair.

A single tear escaped, trailing a silent, wet path down her cheek as she locked her gaze with his, willing him to surrender to what was about to follow. A part of Roland withered and died

*The Ruby Dagger*

a little as he watched. He was unable to turn his eyes away, equally unable to bear the weight of her unspoken goodbye.

"Grace..." Roland said to her, trying to offer what comfort he could as he then forced himself to meet Sir David's eyes. "Let her go. You do not want to do such a thing. I am unarmed, David, and no threat to you." He lifted his empty hands in supplication.

Sir David shook his head heavily, his eyes closing slowly in regret. But Roland could see the burgeoning resolve that was tightening the man's face. The shoulder of his knife arm. He was committed to murder, and only a moment from setting the point firmly and driving it home in the flesh of her neck.

"I cannot. I cannot see any other way out of this," Sir David said, and it was like a prayer for forgiveness.

No. *No.*

Foolish though it was, he leapt for Sir David, his hands outstretched to deflect the attack. To reach her. And that's when Grace hit Sir David with the candlestick, using all the strength of terror she could muster.

Blood blossomed like a line of ruby droplets against the fair skin of her neck, and she fell, shattering his battered heart into a thousand pieces.

Roland all but shoved Sir David aside in his haste to catch her before she hit her head on the shelves, and Grace pushed feebly at him. "I am fine," she murmured, covering the wound on her throat with her left hand. "Leave me. You must stop him. He will be getting away."

"*I do not care about him,*" Roland snarled at her, gathering her to his chest in a panic. "Grace, my God, Grace, let me see." He brushed her hand aside, more afraid than he had ever been, terrified that he would find a mortal wound beneath the white of her glove that was slowly turning red.

The cut was deep enough, but some providence had kept

the knife from nicking that most fragile artery. The flow was still an alarmingly steady seep, but at least she was not dead. Perhaps she had turned just so as she had swung the candlestick. Perhaps David's hand had faltered in the end. He buried his mouth in her hair, uttering a half-sob of gratitude to whatever it had been, even as he pressed his fingers to her throat to stem the bleeding.

"The queen... she will be upset that you let Sir David escape. And you are getting blood all over yourself, Sir Barbarian," Grace murmured with a hint of censure, her breath a soft whisper against the skin of his cheek.

"I do not care about that either," Roland said, but more tenderly this time, and he pressed his forehead to hers as the desperate terror began to wane, and fatigue settled into his bones.

He would have to let her go, for he had no say in the course that had been plotted for his life, and he would be forced to honour it. But for now... for this one moment, he could touch the one he wanted to. For just this moment in time, he would allow himself to wish that things were different.

# 26

If not for the steady drumbeat of pain and the wetness on her hand, Grace would have almost believed the moment to be a dream. Roland lifted his head and brushed a kiss against her forehead. His lips burned against her skin. Grace wanted more from him. She shifted to free her hand and sent a spike of pain across her chest.

Close as he was, Roland caught her sharp inhalation and reared back. "Mind your cut!" He sat up and tugged at his cravat, growling when his fingers caught in the knot. Finally, it came loose. He folded it over and over again and then held it against the cut on her neck. "This will help slow the bleeding."

"Lord Percy?" A deep voice called from outside the room. Boot heels thundered up the stairs.

"Thorne?" Roland asked. "We are in the study."

Thorne burst through the doorway and stopped short at the sight of Grace's bloodied dress.

"She is all right, but for needing to be stitched," Roland assured him. "We must send for a doctor. I do not want to move her, bleeding as she is."

Thorne needed no prodding. He dashed off, shouting an

order, and returned a moment later. "The Greens' butler will see to it. He is keen to prove his innocence in this whole matter."

Grace did not care about the butler at that moment. The pain was a constant reminder of the real villain. "Sir David—"

"He did not make it past his doorstep, my lady," Thorne replied. "I came as soon as I got word. I was considering the best way to get inside, when the man himself threw his front door open and came stumbling out. Blood was streaming down his forehead and into his eyes. I do not think he even knew it was me who had a hold of him until I gave him my name." He glanced at Roland. "Wise of you to knock him in the head. What did you use?"

"A candlestick. And it was Grace who hit him, not I." Roland gave Grace another soft glance. "I am so sorry, Grace. When I think about how things might have ended..."

"You came for me. You got here in time," Grace added. She laid her right hand upon his. "My injury is not so grave that I will not heal. There is no need whatsoever for you to apologise."

Voices called up the stairs, signalling the arrival of more people. True to his word, Sir David's butler showed a man in a dark suit into the study.

"Doctor Simmons, my lady," he explained in a trembling voice. "He runs the surgery at the end of the street."

Grace watched Roland's face, trusting him to assess the competency of the doctor. There was nothing to fear, however. Doctor Simmons set his medical bag on top of the desk and began pulling out the instruments he needed. He offered Roland the bottle of laudanum and a small cap.

"No, none of that," Grace said, holding up a hand to stop Roland. "I will not be delivered home, half insensible or worse. Nor can I remain here. I will bear the pain."

*The Ruby Dagger*

"Grace..." Roland looked fit to be tied between her point and the reality. "It will be painful."

"The young lady makes a fair point," Doctor Simmons said, surprising them both. "I am aware you are not a resident of this street. If you can stand it, I will work as quickly as I can. You should only require a few stitches in the worst parts. The rest will heal with time and the application of a healing salve."

Despite her determination, Grace's breath hitched when she caught sight of the needle and spool of silk thread.

Roland captured her hand and squeezed it. "Do not watch; it will make you nervous. Look at me, Grace. Not at the doctor." He glanced up at the man in question and added a command for the man to heat the needle in the flame of a nearby candle before he set to his task. "I picked up the trick from a surgeon in my unit. He swore it helps keep the wound clean."

The doctor rolled his eyes but did as Roland all but demanded, and she smiled briefly. The man's hint of insolence proved a distraction for Grace at the moment she needed it most. She was lying on the floor of a stranger's home. She dared not think about how much ankle was on display, nor on the state of her dress. Her eyes tracked Roland's every movement, just as he had instructed. He shifted around until he sat on his knees at her side, and then lowered his face until it filled her view.

"Would you like to hear the tale of my first battlefield injury?" he asked, as though they were sitting in her drawing room with cups of tea in their hands. "Thorne was there to bear witness, little help though he proved to be..."

With his strong, rough hand wrapped around hers, he kept up a steady patter while the doctor poked around the wound. A soft cry escaped her lips when the needle first slid through.

Roland raised his voice a notch, commandeering her attention. "I took a knife to my posterior."

That caught her attention. "You *what*? In battle? You did not. You are making up tales."

Thorne coughed a laugh, "No, my lady. This is true. I had nearly forgotten that one."

"I would like to tell you it was heroically received in battle... but that is not the case," Roland admitted, his eyes flickering with amusement. He paused for a moment as she breathed through the next stitch. "I was young—mayhap just eighteen at the time—and both Arion and I were rather green still."

"Like new spring grass," Thorne interrupted.

"Hush, you. You were no better," Roland groused at him, and her smile came easier to hear the two men banter.

"Young Lord Percy cut a fine figure dressed for battle," Thorne continued, "and he certainly knew it, the way he strutted about camp—"

"—Do not listen to him malign my character, or I will tell you about the first day he rode on Horse," Roland whispered close to her ear and she let out a quiet giggle, trying to hold still.

"But how did you get hurt?" she asked.

"I was preparing to mount Arion, and just as I stuck a boot in the stirrup and began to swing astride, some nasty insect stung him right on the snout. A bee, perhaps. I confess, I do not know for sure, for the next thing I knew I was looking at the sky wondering what happened."

"Arion took off like a shot, flinging our lord most unceremoniously for a backward tumble that had him land on his own knife. Cut right through his coat and breeches, my lady," Thorne laughed.

Roland nodded confirmation that it was true.

"Were you badly hurt?" Grace asked.

"Hardly worse than you are. What was the more grievous injury was the one to my pride, for this was the talk of the camp

*The Ruby Dagger*

for weeks after. The surgeon had me stitched up in a thrice—almost as quickly as Doctor Simmons has done for you."

"Indeed," the doctor said. He wrapped a strip of linen round and round until he deemed the wound sufficiently protected. "You must rest, my lady. No balls until the wound is completely healed."

"Even if I desired to dance, my mama will not let me out in this state." Grace made to sit up, but her head spun. Roland got his feet underneath him and then slid his arms under her back and legs. He lifted her up as though she weighed nothing at all.

"I took the liberty of pulling a carriage around to the back of the house, my lord," Thorne said. "We can do the same at the lady's home and none should be the wiser of her foray here."

"Were that I could hope the same for her family," Roland muttered darkly. Though he took great care with his steps, the movement sent stabs of pain through Grace. The bravery that she had shown until then finally escaped her and she swooned right there in Roland's arms.

# 27

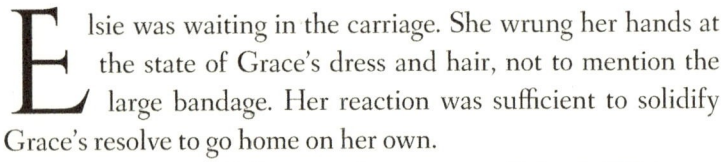

Elsie was waiting in the carriage. She wrung her hands at the state of Grace's dress and hair, not to mention the large bandage. Her reaction was sufficient to solidify Grace's resolve to go home on her own.

"I am fine now," Grace said to reassure Roland. "Elsie can keep watch over me during the ride, and our footmen can assist me with getting inside the house."

Roland set Grace on her feet and then glowered at her. "I do not like the idea of sending you home without an escort."

"Trust me, this is the lesser of all evils. My parents are likely already livid over my running away. It is best if they do not have you there to inflict their fury upon."

"My lady is right," Elsie piped up from the carriage doorway. "The ride is not long, my lord. I will send a message to Mr Thorne later to let you know how she is getting along."

Roland relented in the face of their determination, but only after getting their agreement that Thorne would follow the carriage on his own horse. Only then did he help Grace into the carriage. Elsie bade Grace to rest her head on a cushion on her lap. The carriage ride passed in a haze, and before Grace knew it, they arrived at the stables behind her home. Satisfied they were safe, Thorne turned and went on his way.

"Do not move, my lady," Elsie ordered, taking control over the situation. She bade the stableboy to call the footmen for help. The perpetually curious young lad peered into the gloom of the curtained carriage and caught sight of Grace. He ran off, shouting at the top of his lungs that the young miss was back home and covered in blood.

"Help me down, Elsie," Grace demanded. "If my parents see me lying prone, they will fear the worst."

Elsie, too, saw the wisdom of this change of plans. She waved for Grantham, the Tilbury's carriage driver, to hurry over and offer a hand. Together, they had Grace standing on her own two feet by the time the masses arrived.

Lady Tilbury led the charge, with Lord Tilbury and Felix hot on her heels. Grace nearly laughed at the sight of her mother outracing the footman, with her skirts hiked up high enough to show her ankles.

"I am hale, Mama," Grace announced in vain.

"But not whole!" Lady Tilbury retorted. "My dear baby girl! What has become of you? And where have you been?"

Lord Tilbury's face was beet red above his snow white cravat. It took Grace a moment to figure out that it was because he was crying rather than preparing a rant. "Heavens above, Grace, I feared the worst when your mama said you had disappeared." He motioned for his wife to step clear and allow the footmen to bundle Grace up and carry her to her room.

"I can walk, Father," Grace said, and then promptly swayed on her feet to prove the lie in her words.

It was Felix who swept in and saved Grace from further mortification. He wrapped an arm around her waist to steady her and guided her inside, leaving the others to pose their questions to Elsie. He prodded Grace for information in a low tone as they made their way through the house. "I heard half the palace guard was sent out on a mission, but I did not expect they were sent after my own sister."

"They were not," Grace countered, exhausted. "Though they did go based on information I discovered. We caught a murderer today, but I am not sure whether the guards managed to lay their hands upon the mastermind."

Felix missed a step and nearly sent them both tumbling. Grace grabbed onto the bannister while she waited for Felix to right himself.

"*We?* Murderer? What do you mean by mastermind? And why were you involved?"

Grace brushed his questions aside with a flick of her wrist. "Let's suffice it to say that I did a favour for the queen, and I did not escape entirely unscathed."

Felix's mouth dropped open. When he got it closed, he squinted at her, searching for the lie. "My word! My own sister! How have I been unaware of this?"

Grace let his question linger until they reached her bedroom door. She shrugged off his help and turned back to face him. "Fear not, brother dear. My involvement in such matters has not been part of any discussions. And secret it shall remain, lest you consider loosening your lips." Then she closed the door in his face.

It did not remain closed for more than a minute. Elsie came up fast behind to help her out of her stained dress. Her mama oversaw everything from the centre of the bedroom, alternating between tears of joy at seeing Grace's return, and anguished cries over her injury. When Elsie offered a dose of laudanum, Grace took it gratefully, if for no other reason than to escape the next few hours with her mother.

She woke early the next morning, her neck paining her into

*The Ruby Dagger*

awareness. Elsie rose from the cot in the dressing room where she often slept when Grace was ill.

"How are you this morning, miss?" Elsie asked. She brought over a basin and sponge and set to work cleaning the wound. "The queen sent you a jar of her special healing salve. Imagine that! The queen of all England rousing herself to concern over my lady!"

Elsie held up the jar for Grace to admire. It was a small porcelain jar, round and smooth, with a delicate floral pattern in blues and golds. The lid was topped with an intricate pink rose. The scents of lavender and chamomile filled the air, followed by the delicate sweetness of honey. There was an undertone Grace could not place.

"It's made with myrrh," Elsie explained. "Just like in the Bible!"

Queen Charlotte could not be too cross with Grace if she was willing to send such an extravagant treatment over. Of course, had anyone listened to Grace when she raised her early suspicions of Lady Fitzroy, they might not have ended up in the trouble they did. Although Grace forced herself to admit, Lady Fitzroy was only part of the puzzle. Not a single one of them had a clue about Sir David Green's crucial role in the matter.

Thoughts of Sir David naturally pulled Grace's mind back to the day before. To Roland. "Has anyone else sent word? Or come by?"

"I should hope not!" Elsie reared back. "Your mama will need more than her smelling salts if she finds out society has caught wind of your antics."

A light rap on the door prevented Grace from asking any other question. Grace braced herself to face her mother, but it was Charity who walked into the room. Her dear friend rushed across the room on slippered feet and gasped at the sight of Grace's old bloody bandages.

"He was right to send me to you," Charity cried, making no sense at all.

"Roland?" Grace whispered.

"Mr Thorne," Charity replied. "He sent a note round last night, on behalf of Lord Percy, I imagine, suggesting I call on you today. He asked that I send word back as to your health. Your poor neck! Your mama must be frothing at the risk of a scar."

"I am certain she will be, and will probably ban me from setting foot out of the house for the rest of the season. Please, sit here beside me and keep me company while Elsie finishes her ministrations."

Charity took great care not to jostle Grace as she settled on the foot of the bed. She sat facing Grace so that Grace would not have to turn her head in order to see her. Elsie finished a minute later and left to see about a breakfast tray.

Now alone, Charity asked Grace to tell her all that had happened. Her blue eyes widened as she learned of Lady Fitzroy's arrival at Madame Moreau's, of Grace's fortuitous glimpse of the stolen ruby dagger, and all that happened after.

"You did all that on your own? Hailing a hackney? Visiting a veritable stranger without anyone accompanying you?"

Grace gave a small shrug with her shoulders. "I had no choice, Charity. It was Lady Fitzroy! After all she had done, I could not wait for a chaperone to escort me about town. Of course, had I known I was walking into the home of the murderer, I might have reconsidered my decision. By the time I knew, it was too late."

Charity patted Grace's leg. "You must have been dreadfully afraid, being there alone."

Grace had been terrified, but she had not been without hope. "I counted upon the others to get word to Roland. I had only to survive long enough for him to arrive." When Charity wrinkled her brow, Grace rushed to amend her sentence. "His butler had promised to find him and send him over."

"And Roland," Charity began, saying the name slowly, as though testing its shape in her mouth. "He came to the rescue like a knight of old?"

Grace nodded. "Although, in truth, I proved myself to be rather handy at swinging a candlestick. But even when Sir David made to get away, Roland did not leave my side. He stayed there, caring for my wound, until Sir David's butler found a doctor. I do not think I could have borne the pain had Roland not distracted me while the doctor did his work." Grace's pitch lowered, and she gazed up at the ceiling, seeing not the intricate plasterwork, but instead remembering the warmth of his brown eyes and the way his mouth tipped up on the side when he said something funny.

"Grace? Is something amiss?" Charity asked, recalling Grace to the present.

Grace flushed at being caught daydreaming, and then paled when she realised who sat across from her.

*Roland's intended bride. Her best friend.*

Grace's gut clenched in regret, and fear... and abject sadness. This was not Charity's fault. This was no one's fault. It simply was as it was.

Grace cleared her throat. "You are very fortunate to be marrying Lord Percy. I do not think he will be the type of man to abandon you during your confinement."

Charity held Grace's gaze without blinking. Never before had Grace felt that she was laid bare, all the way to her very soul.

"Are you happy, Grace?"

"Am I what?" Grace caught herself before she shook her head. "I am in bed, with my neck swathed in bandages, and my mama due to harangue me until my ears ring. It is hardly the happiest moment of my life."

"Are you happy with how your season is going?" Charity clarified, still not moving her gaze.

"It has been interesting. Far more than I ever imagined. But as to whether I am enjoying it, when I expressed my interest in new experiences, I dare say I did not wish for the two of us to suffer as we have."

"What of suitors?" Charity said, refusing to move on. "Has anyone caught your eye? You can tell me. We pledged to assist one another, remember?"

Had they made such a pledge? Grace could not recall it if they had. She supposed Charity might have the early days in mind, when they had compared notes on the various possible suitors. But as for Grace giving Charity a hand, other than rescuing her, there had been no cause for her to get involved. Men flocked to Charity.

Yet Charity stared intently at Grace, scrutinising her features for hidden truths. For a moment, Grace feared she had let slip too much. She never intended to give Charity any hint of her sentiment for Roland.

Even now, battered and wounded as she was, Grace did not let her guard drop completely. She thought back to Charity's complaints about Roland. About his inability to express an opinion. His unwillingness to speak of the future. Mayhap he had the right of it.

"I will recover, Charity. Lace collars will hide any scarring. Next season, I will join the dance of courtship, and maybe even allow a man to escort me around the ballroom floor. And you, my dearest friend, will marry. And you will be happy. That is enough for me."

Charity rocked back and cocked her head to the side. She

looked off into the distance. Whatever thoughts passed through her mind stayed secret.

"And you? Are you happy?" Grace asked in a gentle tone. "If Lady Fitzroy made good on her plans to escape, she will not be here to trouble you any longer. By the time she dares to return, assuming that day comes, you will be married and out of her reach."

Charity straightened her head and met Grace's eyes. "Yes, yes I will be. But look at you. You must be famished and suffering. I should not linger, especially as I have another errand to run before I return home. I will call again soon. I promise."

Charity gave Grace's leg a friendly squeeze and then rose from the bed. She smoothed her skirts, took a deep breath, and left with a wave goodbye.

## 28

Roland had expected that the queen would be sending for him sooner rather than later, given that Albert had roused the guard. But it seemed that perhaps she thought he should stew in his thoughts a bit. A request from her staff that he present himself at the palace the next day—early—gave him some notion of the trouble he was in, but still, somehow, it was among the bottom of his list of considerations whirling around his head.

After Thorne left to escort Grace and Elsie back to the Tilbury residence, Roland took his horse home. He had paced around his townhouse like a restless ghost, unable to find peace. Food brought to him lay untouched, and Thorne refused to let Roland send him away.

The morning found him still sitting in a wingback chair he had settled on sometime after midnight. Though he had first been staring out into the darkness, the breaking dawn light brought the lines of his father's dead rear gardens into bas relief.

A soft knock upon the door stirred him out of dark musings, and Thorne stood to answer. "How is he?" Mrs Archer's voice

*The Ruby Dagger*

was soft and low, but in the silence her words carried easily enough.

"Troubled," was all Thorne responded. A clatter of china sounded as a tray was exchanged, and then the door closed again.

"Mrs Archer brought you porridge and fruit," Thorne murmured, setting the tray on the table beside him.

"That was kind of her," Roland replied, but he made no move to avail himself of it.

"Roland, you should eat something. We must prepare you to go to the palace soon," Thorne said, laying his hand on Roland's shoulder.

"I have made a proper mess of things, have I not?" Roland asked him, ignoring the food and getting out of the chair. He moved to the side table where the pitcher stood and washed his face twice, still imagining he saw spots of blood on his skin.

Grace's blood.

"There's nothing there," Thorne reassured him, helping him change clothes. "And no, you have not made such a mess. You saved Lady Grace's life, and that is no small thing. The rest is simply details."

"Details." Rubbing the dull ache pounding in his forehead, Roland said nothing else. How could he? What would he say to Thorne when he barely understood the mire of his thoughts himself?

The streets of London were too-brilliant with sunshine, and he squinted against the blinding light as he sat on horseback. Beyond the discomfort of the light, he paid no attention to the journey.

A few feet ahead of them, Thorne made his way towards the palace, and perhaps sensing his master's mood, Arion was content to follow Horse.

It wasn't until the horses stopped and Thorne called him to

attention that he roused himself once more. "Roland," he said seriously as the palace stableboy led their mounts away. "You have to pull yourself together."

"I know," he replied, and he shook himself, heading into the palace. The things that weighed heavily on his mind now had naught to do with dismissing the needs of the crown, and though they would decide he had erred, he could not find it within himself to be sorry. He would not be sorry for not pursuing Lady Fitzroy, or for nearly allowing Sir David's escape, and he would not enter the palace with the demeanour of a wayward servant bracing for a whipping.

The footman took him through St James's halls—not to the throne room, as he half expected, but to an audience room. The better for his formal castigation, he supposed.

Queen Charlotte and Prinny were already seated and waiting when he arrived, and their expressions were forbidding. Roland approached the pair with his eyes properly downcast, and he made a deep bow, acknowledging their authority. But when he stood up again, he met the eyes of the queen in the briefest show of defiance before averting his gaze, awaiting their recognition.

"Lord Percy," Queen Charlotte said by way of greeting, "if I did not know better, I would assume from your appearance that you've spent the night carousing in the gutters rather than preparing for this audience."

"Forgive me, Your Majesty, if I found sleep somewhat difficult to find after yesterday's events."

"*Events,* I suppose, would be one way of putting it," Prinny replied, taking the reins from his mother. "One full third of the standing guard dispatched—and on the word of your butler, no less—while we were in the middle of a state ceremony certainly proved quite eventful!"

"And your 'messenger' came too late to catch Lady Fitzroy.

*The Ruby Dagger*

She made the journey to Gravesend, and the boat was at sea a full hour before our forces could get there!" the queen's voice cracked like a whip through the audience room.

"Did your men learn where the ship was bound?" Roland dared to ask them.

"Easily. She boarded the ambassador's ship," Prinny said, shifting forward in his seat. "Were you aware of any sort of plotting between the two of them?"

"Directly between Lady Fitzroy and the ambassador? No, I was not," Roland said. "But as you acknowledged before, there was some degree of kinship between them. I did, however, chance to witness Lord Peregrine Fitzroy meet with Lindberg at White's."

There was a murmur of low conversation between the two royals, too low for him to make out, and a peculiar sensation flitted through Roland. "Was Fitzroy aboard that ship in Gravesend as well?"

"The reports were that only the dowager Lady Fitzroy and her daughter Lark boarded that ship in Gravesend. Lord Fitzroy was not mentioned, and neither were we able to find him at his places of residence in London," Prinny murmured, settling himself back in his chair again.

The queen waved the matter of Peregrine off. "He is his mother's pawn at best, and we will deal with him. But letting the mastermind behind the scheme escape—" the queen's face coloured with her displeasure, her voice trailing off. "I would rather like to hear it from you, in your words, why you decided that this message was not important enough to bring it to us yourself, with all haste."

This, he knew, would be the sticking point. The tip of the sword that the queen would wield against him. The royals would never admit to their portion of the blame for what happened, so Roland expected nothing less than that he would serve as the outlet to their frustration. He straightened again, folding his hands together behind his back.

Looking the queen once more in the eye as he answered. "Because, Your Majesty, once I found that Lady Grace was heading unwittingly into the lair of the man who committed the murder, there was nothing more important than safeguarding her life."

Prinny frowned deeper, but the queen's brows shifted from supreme irritation to a more displeased thoughtfulness. She let Roland match her gaze as she tested his mettle for a moment, before he turned aside again.

"We thank you for your assistance in revealing the perpetrator and the blackguard in our service, even if it seems that you stumbled across the truth like a blindfolded ox trapped within a china shop," Prinny said formally.

The queen's pause was long. "Yes. I would also like to commend you in the aid you rendered to the young lady. Although I think, Lord Percy, you may be less reliable in your assistance than I previously anticipated. You may go now."

Summarily dismissed, Roland bowed again and backed away to leave. The door closing behind him echoed with a hollow sound, and the skin between his shoulders itched in foreboding. It was done, and there was nothing more for it.

The faint click of footsteps approached, but his body was slow to resume the motion of departure. And so that was how he found himself suddenly face to face with Lady Charity, being escorted to the receiving room by a footman.

He blinked, confused. "My lady? Have you been summoned for some reason?"

After making a small nod to the footman that everything was in order and he might leave them for a moment, Lady Charity stepped closer to him. "No, I was the one who requested an audience, Lord Percy."

*The Ruby Dagger*

Fuddled from the lack of sleep, he could not imagine why. The set of her face was both closed and compassionate, and it stirred a more primordial unease within him than his summons to court had. A hundred questions galloped through his thoughts at once. "Is something wrong with Grace?" he asked, afraid of the answer.

She studied his expression calmly, looking deep within his eyes as if seeking the thoughts that lay beneath the surface. "No. I am just from her house. She is—as well as one could hope for at this juncture. So far, there is no trace of mortification, but her mother is more upset about the fact that when it heals, it will leave a scar."

Roland let his lashes flutter closed for a moment to ease the grainy feel beneath his lids. "I see," was all he could think of to say.

"Do you plan to visit?" was Lady Charity's next question. "She is well enough for that."

"I—I do not think that would be wise," he admitted, and tried to deflect from the truth with some humour. "If nothing else, her father may try to take my head. But it eases my mind a great deal to hear from you that... she is..."

His throat closed with emotion, and after a moment, Lady Charity reached out to set her hand upon his, offering comfort. Looking away, she nodded, as if coming to some sort of decision. "Roland," she finally said, taking a small breath, "I am cancelling our engagement. That is why I have come to see the queen."

In the midst of everything else, her words were so unexpected that he staggered, and he had to put one hand to the wall in the end to keep his balance. "What? Why?"

She grasped his arm to steady him. "You offered me a safe harbour in the storm that overtook my life, and for that... I am so grateful to you for that kindness you offered without question.

But... How could I possibly use that invitation, knowing it would rob you of happiness?"

"Lady Charity—" he said, regaining some of his composure. "I know that we have stumbled, trying to find ground in common, but I do not understand. You do not make me unhappy."

A small line of consternation formed between her eyes as she smiled at him. "That is a relief," she said lightly, "although I am not sure if I entirely believe you. I cannot imagine being so blind as to ignore the fact that you do not want to marry me."

"That does not matter. You should not suffer because of Lady Fitzroy," he said, frowning. "It was not your fault, and it was the most expedient way to fix the issue."

She dropped her hand, looking exasperated, before she finally smiled again—this time more wryly and more genuinely than before. "Of course it matters, you ninny. What sort of person would I be if went ahead in wedding you, knowing it prevented you from marrying someone you love?"

Lightning coursed the length of Roland's spine, and he suddenly found it difficult to breathe. To make any sense of her words.

Love? What—?

With a scowl, Charity smacked him on the shoulder with her fan. "My goodness, Roland. You *do* love Grace, do you not?"

## 29

Between her need to rest and her mother's desire to punish her, Grace did not leave her bedroom for a full week. Elsie brought in her meals on trays. Her father softened enough to allow the footman to take Grace the previous day's newspaper. Felix made a few attempts to get more information from her, but soon abandoned his task.

Apart from two people outside of her family, nobody was aware that she had been hurt. So no one visited her to ease her in her convalescence. Charity, at least, offered an explanation via a note saying her family would be away from town.

From Roland, there was only silence.

Well, that was not entirely true. As she spent time staring out the window in her bedroom, heartily bored, Grace discovered he had begun the habit of walking past every afternoon. He passed by always at the same hour, a time when Elsie was conveniently occupied elsewhere in the house.

After the fifth such event, Grace cornered Elsie and demanded the truth. "Have you seen Lord Percy?"

Elsie blushed and stammered a no. She was a terrible liar.

"So that is why he comes by. Are you speaking with him?"

"Only for a moment, miss. He asks how you are. I assure him you are recovering."

"I see." Grace filed that away until the following day. She slipped down the back stairs, taking care to avoid the housekeeper, the butler, and anyone else who might give her 'adventure' away to her mama. She found Elsie standing at the side gate and pointed her back inside. "I will give my own update to Lord Percy today," she said frostily.

"He knocks twice. That's his signal." Elsie scooted backwards and left her, knowing better than to argue with her mistress when she was using that tone of voice.

Standing alone, Grace felt suddenly awkward. She smoothed the muslin of her day dress and paced up and down the garden path. She did not notice the perfume of the roses or the warm summer sun. Her full attention was on the wooden gate separating her from the rest of the world.

A decisive knock broke her concentration. Then another. It had to be him. Without any hesitation, she flipped the latch and swung open the gate.

Roland indeed stood on the other side of it, dapperly dressed in a pale grey silk tailcoat and black trousers, and looking flustered by the rising summer heat. Or perhaps he was flustered because Grace was standing there, one eyebrow raised archly, instead of her maid as he expected.

"Grace?" he asked, as if uncertain it was really her.

"Were you expecting someone else, *Roland?*" she said, unaccountably furious at him, and she was not quite certain why. Wait—she did know. Instead of calling on her to see how she was doing, he had skulked around, interrogating Elsie. He had not come to see her, and it hurt.

But the smile that lit his face made her fury with him waver, and so she reminded herself of the fact again. He had *not* come to see her. The urge to castigate him for his behaviour here and

*The Ruby Dagger*

now was overwhelming, but she latched a hand on his arm and all but dragged him into the garden. She closed the gate and made sure it latched, not wanting an audience for his dressing down.

"Follow me," she stated boldly, and then set off on a pebbled path. She arrived at a small wooden bench and sat on it, leaving him to stand. "As you can see, I am fully recovered, so you may cease pestering my maid for information. Should you wish to learn anything else about me, you shall have to pay a call like the rest of the ton. Unless, that is, you can offer another explanation for your noted silence."

Roland's face grew serious. "I am unsurprised to find you are angry with me, but how would I explain my visit to your mama? How would I explain how I learned you were unwell? I must assume you did not tell your parents that I saw you get hurt or brought you home."

"You could have at least sent a note," she said, unable to keep a hint of petulance out of her voice.

His eyes softened with regret. "I... You are right. I should have given Elsie at least some word. Sent you some note."

"Yes, you should have. My father gives me day-old sheets, and though I scoured them from front to back, I found no news of what transpired. Not a peep about Sir David, nor the ambassador and the stolen dagger. It has been driving me to distraction and I am entirely wroth with you for not keeping me apprised of what has happened!"

He sighed, rubbing the back of his head. "Lady Fitzroy remains at large, after a successful escape. We think she sailed for Sweden with the ambassador, although if they stop along the way, she could go anywhere."

"What of the rest of the family?" She looked confused. "Did Lord Fitzroy and Lady Lark not go along?"

"Lady Lark did indeed accompany her mother, but

Peregrine remained behind. He nearly ended up in the tower, though, and has decided to join Wellington's troops on the continent. He said he means to prove his loyalty to the crown."

Grace contemplated his response, but questions lingered. "Was there something to indicate Lord Fitzroy was involved? He has been helpful to us in the past, and he did not have any knowledge of his mother's actions with regard to Charity."

"The knife used to kill the guard—the one that Sir David wielded against you—we were finally able to examine it properly. We found the Fitzroy crest hidden underneath the leather wrapping."

Grace's eyes widened. "It was Lord Fitzroy's dagger? No wonder he became a suspect. How did he clear his name?"

"Fitzroy did not. It was Sir David Green who made a full confession from his cell in the Tower. He provided testimony of Lady Fitzroy's involvement in exchange for the promise of clemency for Matthew, and explained he took the knife from the Fitzroy home to use as leverage should the dowager think to double cross him. Not that it did him any good. He was as in the dark about her plans to escape England as everyone else. With her in the wind, Sir David is left to take the blame for it all."

"What will happen to Sir David now?"

"I have heard nothing formal, but given the secrecy around the matter, I doubt it will go to trial. It would be easier for all involved if he met his fate in a... more private manner," Roland said softly, and Grace blanched as she understood his meaning.

"I suppose that is that, then, although it still makes my skin crawl to think Lady Fitzroy is still free," she murmured.

"Then perhaps we should move on to less disturbing matters, since there is little else we can do about her until she rears her head again. If she does. Let us hope she has gone to ground and will stay hidden in some far away kingdom so that we never have to worry about it again."

*The Ruby Dagger*

"And you and Charity can finally celebrate your happily ever after?" she asked, trying to lift one corner of her mouth in a smile, but it seemed pained. "I had a note from Charity that she was leaving town. Is she off making wedding preparations?"

Roland's face shifted through a sea-change of emotion, ending in uncertain regret. "Ah, no. Lady Charity decided to end our engagement the very next day, after she visited you. She... she did not tell you?"

"She did *what*?" Grace gasped. "But... Whatever for?"

"She knew I did not wish to marry her," he said simply, looking embarrassed and uncomfortable.

Any lingering anger fled from Grace, and she felt sorry for him. She shifted down the bench in silent invitation. "Is anyone else aware of this information?"

Seeing the space, he sat beside her, giving her a weak smile. "It is not common knowledge, but I am not sure how far the news has travelled. I thought for certain she would have at least told you and your family, which was the other reason I stayed away. Otherwise, your father and brother would have either shown up on my doorstep demanding satisfaction for ruining you, or to rush us to the altar."

Grace was so baffled by the picture of being rushed to the altar with him, she did not have a clue what to say. Finally, she latched onto the memory of Charity's last visit. "I am so sorry she ended things. I did not say anything to her about your feelings towards her—you must believe me, Roland."

"It was nothing you said or did," he said, touching her hand in reassurance. "If anything, the fault was mine."

"What are you going to do now?" she asked hesitantly. "This must upset the apple cart for you, because you said that you had to marry this season, did you not?"

"At my grandfather's insistence," he admitted. "But I have come to realise you were right, when you said I was reluctant to want more for myself. I have seldom ever had the luxury of making plans of my own, and I am ready for that to change. I learned the hard cost of allowing others to dictate my future. For my next courtship, I will make my own choice and allow my heart some say in the matter."

"Oh?" Grace asked in a near whisper. A band of tension wrapped around her chest, and she hardly dared to breathe. "Is your heart drawing you in any direction?"

"That depends," Roland said. He cupped her chin until he could look her in the eye. "Where do you intend to spend the summer, Lady Grace?"

"My family is going to Brighton." She took a deep breath and then added, "I hear it is lovely this time of year. If you want... you could join us."

Roland and Grace will be back again in THE SAPPHIRE INTRIGUE.

**A stolen code, a locked-down Pavilion, and a love on the line—Regency Brighton's season of secrets is just beginning.**

*Brighton, 1813:* The upper class exchanges London's bustling streets for the serene seaside elegance of the Royal Pavilion. A summer of relaxation and romance beckons, especially for Lord Roland Percy and Lady Grace Tilbury.

Yet, tranquillity is shattered when a key military advisor is found murdered, and his secret military codes stolen, plunging the Prince Regent into a frenzy. Under royal edict, the Pavilion is locked down, leaving Roland and Grace with a daunting

*The Ruby Dagger*

ultimatum: recover the missing codes or forfeit the royal favour on their budding courtship.

The investigation seems straightforward, with just a few likely suspects. But the mystery deepens when their top suspect meets a similarly grim fate, forcing them to question everything they thought they knew. As they navigate a labyrinth of deceit, the traitor they seek slips further from their grasp.

With time running out, Roland and Grace are thrust into a desperate hunt to catch the traitor before he disappears with the tides. Their future together, and the very security of the British Empire, are at stake.

**Can they expose the villain, or will their inaugural season in Brighton also be their last?**

Find out in THE SAPPHIRE INTRIGUE. You can order it now on Amazon.

∽

Want to keep updated on our newest books? Subscribe to Lynn's newsletter for book news, sales, special offers, and great reading recommendations. You can sign up here: LINK

# Historical Notes

In preparation for writing this book, we dove into the historical record in search of inspiration. We knew we needed a villain related to the military and an ambassador to visit to kick things off. As always, history came through with plenty of inspiration. Although we took certain liberties with the creation of our imaginary characters, we thought you might be interested to learn more about the real people we uncovered during our research.

Despite his lack of book time, the ambassador was one of the more difficult characters to sort out. We went through three different name changes and countries of origin for the man while we did research.

Originally, we were thinking of a region in Germany, but in 1813, the German Confederation was a patchwork of territories and states. It was an utter hodgepodge of foreign policy, and a dark rabbit hole of research trying to find a suitable place of origin for him. We wanted the relationship between Britain and the ambassador's country of origin to be somewhat tumultuous —if not downright poor. Enter Sweden, which was then one unified kingdom (more or less).

*Historical Notes*

Like many areas that had built an industry of trade, they suffered a great deal economically in the Napoleonic wars. A large part of this was due to the Continental System, the maritime blockade Britain imposed on France and its allies starting in 1806. Napoleon countered with his own embargo, forbidding import of British goods into European countries allied with or dependant on France, and much of the global trade system broke down throughout Europe.

At that time, Sweden was ruled by King Gustav IV Adolf, who aligned closely with Britain and Russia's anti-France stances. Unfortunately for Gustav IV, Russia was soon after defeated by Napoleon at the Battle of Friedland. The Treaty of Tilsit, signed in 1807, meant that Russia changed their allegiance to France. The next year, Russia attacked Sweden in the Finnish war (1808-1809), and in the aftermath, they took Finland away from Sweden.

Britain and Sweden's relationship was somewhat complicated on both sides because for a while Sweden had tried to be neutral. While there was no specific aid promised to Sweden by the British, there are some hints that Britain implied some kind of common interest support to countries who opposed Napoleon's embargo. But nothing formal, however, developed until after the Finnish War.

After losing the Finnish War and Finland, Gustav IV was deposed in a coup. His uncle, Charles XIII, ascended the throne. However, Charles XIII was elderly and childless, and his first adopted heir apparent died. In 1810, Charles XIII adopted Jean Baptiste Bernadotte, one of Napoleon's former marshals, as the Crown Prince of Sweden. Bernadotte changed his name to Karl Johan, and by 1813 and the time of the book, he was regent. Charles XIII was still alive, but infirm.

You might be wondering if a former French marshal becoming regent and later King Charles XIV worked in

*Historical Notes*

Napoleon's favour. It did not, although he hoped it would extend his influence. Instead, Bernadotte joined the Sixth Coalition forces fighting Napoleon. He transitioned from a French marshal to a Swedish royal, and the House of Bernadotte still rules Sweden today.

As for our villain, it was a small mention on Wikipedia showing a gap in Prince Frederick's service record that set our minds spinning. Prince Frederick, Duke of York and Albany (Frederick Augustus; 16 August 1763 – 5 January 1827) was the second son of King George III and Queen Charlotte. As the spare, he spent his professional career leading the military, up to and including acting as the Commander-in-Chief of the British Army during the wars against Napoleon. His service record is impressive, as is his legacy in restructuring the army. We writers, however, were more interested in a small gap in his record as Commander-in-Chief.

From 25 March 1809 until 29 May 1811, General Sir David Dundas had to step in as a sort of interim head of the British Forces when a bribery scandal forced Prince Frederick to resign. Frederick's mistress, a one Mary Anne Clarke, was accused of illegally selling army commissions, under the auspices of having Frederick's permission to do so. It took two years for information to come to light that would exonerate Frederick of any hint of the scandal.

Mary Anne Clarke (nee Thompson) began life as the daughter of a tradesman. At 18, she wed one Mr Clarke, a stonemason, but their relationship proved unstable. When Clarke declared bankruptcy, Mary Anne sought other avenues for income. She worked her way into becoming an established courtesan, thanks to her beauty, and eventually caught the eye of King George's second son. For his part, Frederick's affection for his mistress outsized his pocketbook. When he failed to give

*Historical Notes*

her enough funds to pay for their lifestyle, she turned to selling the aforementioned army commissions.

Before splitting with her husband, Mary Anne had one daughter — Ellen Clarke. Ellen married Louis-Mathurin Busson du Maurier. Their son was the caricaturist George du Maurier, and their great-granddaughter was the novelist Daphne du Maurier, who immortalised her great-great-grandmother with her book *Mary Anne*.

We wanted to fit much more of Frederick and Mary Anne's story into The Ruby Dagger, but it proved to be too complex to fit in with the remainder of the plans. We kept the image of the temporary replacement in mind, wondering what would happen to a military leader of that level when the Crown no longer had use for him. From there, we invented the character of Sir David Green. His actions and words are solely the product of our imaginations.

# Acknowledgments

Thanks to Melody Simmons for creating various drafts of the cover for this book in an effort to get it just right.

Thanks to Brenda Chapman, Jody Tappan, Ken Morrison, and Lois King for acting as beta readers. We are grateful for their willingness to deal with typos and provide feedback on the story.

As always, we want to give a warm shout-out to our Advance Reader Team for their generosity of time in reading early copies and providing timely reviews. Additionally, we would not be here if not for all the people who took a chance on a pair of cowriters and gave this series of ours a try.

# The Sapphire Intrigue
## A Crown Jewels Regency Mystery

**A stolen code, a locked-down Pavilion, and a love on the line—Regency Brighton's season of secrets is just beginning.**

*Brighton, 1813:* The upper class departs London's bustling streets for the serene seaside elegance of the Royal Pavilion. A summer of relaxation and romance beckons, especially for Lord Roland Percy and Lady Grace Tilbury.

Yet, tranquillity is shattered when a key military advisor is found murdered, and his secret military codes stolen, plunging the Prince Regent into a frenzy. Under royal edict, the Pavilion is locked down, leaving Roland and Grace with a daunting ultimatum: recover the missing codes or forfeit the royal favour on their budding courtship.

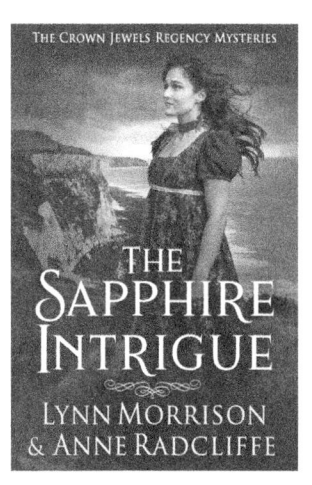

The investigation seems straightforward, with just a few

*The Sapphire Intrigue*

likely suspects. But the mystery deepens when their top suspect meets a similarly grim fate, forcing them to question everything they thought they knew. As they navigate a labyrinth of deceit, the traitor they seek slips further from their grasp.

With time running out, Roland and Grace are thrust into a desperate hunt to catch the traitor before he disappears with the tides. Their future together, and the very security of the British Empire, are at stake.

**Can they expose the villain, or will their inaugural season in Brighton also be their last?**

Find out in THE SAPPHIRE INTRIGUE. You can order it now on Amazon.

# About Anne Radcliffe

As an American Expat living in Ontario with a husband and teen son, Anne Radcliffe spends a lot of time editing or writing in order to avoid having to become a Maple Leafs fan. Anne loves a great story no matter the genre or medium - books, graphic novels, TV, movies or video games. You can find out more about Anne on her website at AnneRadcliffe.com.

- bookbub.com/authors/anne-radcliffe
- goodreads.com/anneradcliffe
- amazon.com/stores/author/B0D1VMVDZ1

# About Lynn Morrison

Lynn Morrison lives in Oxford, England along with her husband, two daughters and two cats. Born and raised in Mississippi, her wanderlust attitude has led her to live in California, Italy, France, the UK, and the Netherlands. Despite having rubbed shoulders with presidential candidates and members of parliament, night-clubbed in Geneva and Prague, explored Japanese temples and scrambled through Roman ruins, Lynn's real life adventures can't compete with the stories in her mind.

She is as passionate about reading as she is writing, and can almost always be found with a book in hand. You can find out more about her on her website LynnMorrisonWriter.com.

You can chat with her directly in her Facebook group - Lynn Morrison's Not a Book Club - where she talks about books, life and anything else that crosses her mind.

- facebook.com/nomadmomdiary
- instagram.com/nomadmomdiary
- bookbub.com/authors/lynn-morrison
- goodreads.com/nomadmomdiary
- amazon.com/Lynn-Morrison/e/B00IKC1LVW

Made in the USA
Las Vegas, NV
04 December 2024